Edward Bean Underhill

Alfred Saker, Missionary to Africa

A biography

Edward Bean Underhill

Alfred Saker, Missionary to Africa
A biography

ISBN/EAN: 9783744757294

Printed in Europe, USA, Canada, Australia, Japan

Cover: Foto ©Raphael Reischuk / pixelio.de

More available books at **www.hansebooks.com**

ALFRED SAKER,

Missionary to Africa:

A BIOGRAPHY.

BY

EDWARD BEAN UNDERHILL, LL.D.,

Honorary Secretary of the Baptist Missionary Society.

PUBLISHED BY THE BAPTIST MISSIONARY SOCIETY,
19, CASTLE STREET, HOLBORN, E.C.,
AND
ALEXANDER & SHEPHEARD, LONDON.

1884.

LONDON:
PRINTED BY ALEXANDER AND SHEPHEARD,
LONSDALE BUILDINGS, CHANCERY LANE.

Paul's love of Christ, and steadiness unbribed,
Were copied close in him, and well transcribed.
He followed Paul : his zeal a kindred flame,
His apostolic charity the same.
Like him, cross'd cheerfully tempestuous seas,
Forsaking country, kindred, friends, and ease :
Like him, he laboured, and, like him, content
To bear it, suffer'd shame where'er he went.

COWPER.

PREFACE.

———

ALFRED SAKER wished to be known under no other designation than a "Missionary to Africa"; and it is under that aspect of his character that the following pages have been compiled. All the energies of his nature were concentrated on that one object, and its fulfilment he held to constitute his one claim to our regard. But in other respects he was a man worthy of admiration and of the deepest affection; and in the pursuit of his aim he never forgot the claims of family love, of Christian duty, or of the Master to whom with great joy he gave the life he had received at His hands. For the purposes of this biography, I have been much indebted to Mrs. Saker for many details of her husband's early life; and the Committee of the Baptist Missionary Society, whose honoured servant he was, have freely placed at my command the correspondence in their hands. A comparison with some pages of the *Missionary Herald* will show that I have freely used many statements recorded there; but as they were the production of my own pen, and often derived from my own personal knowledge, I have not thought it necessary to make any distinct reference to the paragraphs I have quoted or used.

I trust that, under the Divine Blessing, this sketch of a noble and useful life will contribute to deepen the interest of the Christian Church in Foreign Missions, and more particularly in the salvation of that great Continent which still so lamentably needs the utmost devotion of the people of the Lord.

EDWARD B. UNDERHILL.

HAMPSTEAD, *Feb. 5th, 1884.*

CONTENTS.

CHAPTER I.

CHAPTER II.

CHAPTER III.

CHAPTER IV.

CHAPTER IX.

Claim of Spain to Fernando Po—The missionaries driven
away—The Mission abandoned—Exploration of Amboises Bay
—Description—Colony of Victoria founded—Its advantages
—The exiles—Laws of the colony—The home of freedom—
Grateful retrospect.

CHAPTER X.

Progress of the work—Composition of hymns and tunes—
Visit of Mr. Diboll and Mr. Saker to England—Approval of
the Committee—Return voyage—Trials of the Mission—
Intense activity of Mr. Saker—Completion of New Testament
—Classes for reading—Native quarrels—The Dualla language
and people.

CHAPTER XI.

The start—The native population—The ascent—Encampment
—Traces of volcanic action—The summit—Final ascent by
Captain Burton—Return to Victoria.

CHAPTER XII.

Slow growth of Victoria—Description of it—Departure of his
family for England—Interruptions from native quarrels—
Savage life—Attempts to revive the slave trade—Additions to
the church—Failure of health—Another visit to England.

CHAPTER XIII.

Return voyage to Africa—State of Mission—Death of Mrs.
Smith—Perseverance in manifold labours—Death of Johnson
—Obstruction from wars—Progress in translation—Danger of
drowning—Growth of the work—Translation of Bible completed—Baptisms—Visit to England.

CHAPTER XIV.

CHAPTER XV.

CHAPTER XVI.

APPENDIX.

ILLUSTRATIONS.

ALFRED SAKER.

A BIOGRAPHY.

CHAPTER I.

EARLY LIFE AND CONSECRATION, 1814-1842.

HE small hamlet of Borough Green, in the parish of Wrotham, Kent, was the birthplace of Alfred Saker. It lies in a richly cultivated district, below the chalk cliffs that rise to the north, from whence may be seen, looking over the quiet village of Wrotham, one of the most beautiful of the many lovely landscapes that the weald of Kent offers to the lovers of scenery. It is a district of meadows, cornfields, and hop-gardens, interspersed with shaws and orchards. Near at hand are the fine plantations and woods surrounding Mereworth Castle. Still nearer to the little Green, on the north-west, is Addington, with its numerous memorials of Druidical times in circles, broken cromlechs, and the remains of a great stone avenue that remind the traveller of the monumental lines of Carnac in Brittany.

Not far from Borough Green, to the west, is the considerable village of Ightham, with its interesting relics

of the Roman occupation, consisting of a large intrench-
ment and traces of a Roman road, which appears to
have run through Borough Green itself.

Here Alfred Saker was born on the 21st July, 1814,
and amid these scenes he spent the years of his childhood. His father was a millwright and engineer, and
the parent of a large family of children, many of whom
died in infancy. Alfred was a weakly babe, and, in the
opinion of the old nurse, " was not worth rearing." He
grew an exceedingly sensitive child, a gentle, retiring
boy, feeble in frame and caring little for the boisterous
games of the children that gave life to the quiet
village. The only school his parents could afford to
send him to was the National School of the place. He
early showed a great love for books, and preferred their
society to that of his playmates on the Green. At ten
years of age he had mastered all the lessons of the
school, and had made besides good progress in arith-
metic and in the geometry of Euclid. He therefore left,
and soon after entered his father's workshop, carrying
with him an eager thirst for knowledge, filling every
leisure hour with study, and spending every spare penny
in acquiring the books and instruments he longed to
possess.

Among other acquisitions, he learnt to sing. He had
a sweet voice, which he generally exercised in the choir
of Ightham church; but he often accompanied his
choral companions to Wrotham, where the father of his
future wife was the leader of the church's song. Before
he was fifteen years of age, he had purchased a large
pair of globes, which, at a later period, he gave to the
Society of which he became an honoured missionary;
they are now preserved in the library of the Mis-

sion House. A telescope was also among the scientific treasures he dearly loved, and with which he spent hours in the fields behind his father's house till long after midnight, watching the stars. Before he was sixteen, he had constructed a small steam-engine, which remained in his possession till he sold it on the eve of his departure for Africa.

All these incidents of Alfred Saker's youth are eminently characteristic of the man he became, and in the Providence of God his self-chosen pursuits were the most useful preparation that could have been devised for his future career.

Up to this time Alfred Saker's mind does not appear to have been awake to the claims of the Gospel on his faith and love. They had probably never been pressed on his attention. There was, indeed, a small Baptist chapel in the hamlet, which, however, it is likely he had never entered. The people attending it were poor and despised, and the good old minister, the Rev. John Morris, was much persecuted. The small community over which Mr. Morris watched had been formed in 1809, and for twenty-one years he held the office of its Pastor. In 1830 he was removed by death, and was followed in his ministry by the Rev. Wm. Bolton. Mr. Bolton was a man of much energy and singular zeal, and his coming was followed by a revival in the congregation.

It was about this time that Mr. Saker was "lent" by his father to assist in a millwright's business in Sevenoaks. One Sabbath evening he was strolling alone through the street, when the singing in a chapel that he passed drew his attention. He entered. The excellent pastor, the Rev. Thos. Shirley, was not, however, the

1*

preacher, but some stranger. The words to which the
youth listened fastened on his susceptible mind, and
the quiet hours of the night that followed witnessed the
consecration of his life to the service and the kingdom
of his Saviour. The preacher's name he never knew,
nor probably was the fact of Mr. Saker's conversion,
through his sermon, ever made known to him; but, in
after-years, Mr. Saker often referred to the incident as
an encouragement to earnest labourers in Christ's vineyard, who yet may remain ever ignorant of the effect
that their work, under God's blessing, may have
wrought. He soon returned home, and at once became a
teacher in Mr. Bolton's Sunday-school, and shortly after
its superintendent. He assisted in the choir, and as his
gifts drew attention, he was prompt to exercise them in
the cottages and hamlets around. He took an active
part in every good work. Though modest and unas-
suming in manner, he did not fail to exhibit that
firmness and persistency of character which, in later
years, shone out so fully. In a recent reminiscence of
these days, a life-long friend says of him : " What is
most memorable to me now, was the earnestness of his
devotion, and of his pleadings with God at the prayer-
meetings. So much was this the case that I seem to
hear, even now, his earnest tones, although more than
forty years have passed away." On the 4th January,
1834, when nearly twenty years of age, he was baptized
by Mr. Fremling, of Footscray, and became a member of
the church in the village of his nativity.

With the public devotion of himself to Christ, he
began to extend his labours in every direction. His
evenings were either given to self-improvement or he
would go to some member's house, where a few lowly

people were gathered for converse and prayer. His fitness for evangelistic service became more and more apparent. Not a village or hamlet in the neighbourhood was left untouched by his zealous ministrations. "The first time," says the friend already referred to, "that I remember going with him was to Wrotham Common. This, perhaps, may be regarded as the beginning of his ministry. It was a voluntary movement on his part, but most cordially approved by his brethren. At Platt, Ightham, among. the huts of the sand diggers on Wrotham Common, and at other places of the neighbourhood, he sought and found opportunities to carry on the good work." The church soon called him to exercise his ministry in a more formal way, and for some time, at their request, he occupied every other Sabbath the little chapel at Plaxtol.

The death of his father, in 1838, led Mr. Saker to decide on seeking employment elsewhere. He accordingly applied at various dockyards, and, after passing his examination at Woolwich, he was appointed to a situation in Devonport. In his studies for the examination he obtained valuable assistance from the late Rev. Jno. Cox, of Woolwich. His work at the Devonport yard chiefly consisted in the preparation of drawings for the Admiralty. They were of sufficient excellence to secure his promotion on the first vacancy. In October, 1839, he was sent for nine months to the dockyard at Deptford, to superintend the erection of machinery.

In the following month of February, he was married to Miss Helen Jessup, and at the close of his engagement at Deptford, he returned to Devonport.

In the early days of his Christian life, he had

formed the desire to consecrate his powers to the
service of Christ in Africa, but he was more especially stirred at this period to offer himself for this
work by the striking narratives of the Rev. John
Clarke and Dr. Prince, on their return from a visit
of exploration to the West Coast, in the year 1842.
In this wish he was encouraged by his devoted
wife. The counsel and opinion of his highly esteemed
pastor, the Rev. Thos. Horton, brought decision to the
yearnings of his heart, and, after some delay, he was
accepted by the Committee of the Baptist Missionary
Society.   He owed much to the ministry of Mr.
Horton. Writing many years after to Mrs. Horton, on
the decease of her husband, Mr. Saker thus speaks of
the benefit that he received during the years of his
connection with him:—" I shall ever remember the
debt I owe to the departed. In my early days he
showed me the beauty of holiness in a devoted human
life, and also by his teaching and counsel incited all
my affections and faculties in earnest efforts to promote
the present and future happiness of the human family.
And in whatever respect my life in Africa has been a
blessing, it has resulted greatly from the teaching of
those early days, even as the harvest from the seed
sown.   Oft I meditated writing to him while yet
among us on earth—my attempts were failures.   I
wanted to give him a brief account of the result, through
his help, of my life's toil,—in a written language, a
completed Bible, the conversion of hundreds, the training
of young men to teach and to preach, and the gathering
together of churches to maintain the ordinances of
divine service ; thus securing, as far as human eye can
see, the dissemination of the word of God with all its

benign influences. Such lines have never been written; the pleasure to me to tell, and the departed to hear, was denied. I could neither write nor travel. May the mercies of God be long continued to you and yours in this life, and, finally, the joy of endless life with the holy above."

Mr. Saker's residence in Devonport was a period of useful preparation for his missionary career, and he found in his connection with the church in Morrice Square, a fitting sphere for the exercise of his gifts. Old scholars still living, tell of his labours in the Sunday-school with devout thankfulness, and speak with tears of gratitude of his strenuous exertions for their highest welfare.

CHAPTER II.

AMONGST the earliest results in Jamaica of the great Act of Emancipation, was the earnest desire of numbers of the freed Africans to convey the Gospel to the land of their fathers. Many still remembered the homes from which they had been torn, and longed to revisit the place of their birth to communicate the "riches of mercy," of which they had become the grateful recipients in the house of their bondage. Encouraged by numerous offers of personal service, and by the abounding liberality of the Jamaica churches, the Committee of the Baptist Missionary Society, mindful of the Divine blessing that had crowned its labours with such large success in the chief island of the Antilles, felt itself compelled, in its year of Jubilee, to undertake this arduous enterprise. The time was auspicious, and the triumph of freedom over slavery could not more signally or gratefully be commemorated than by an effort to give the light of life to that "Dark Continent," and to atone for the crimes that English greed had for centuries committed, by proclaiming in Africa itself the glad tidings of a Divine liberty from on high.

It was at once seen to be indispensable that fuller information than was then accessible should be obtained,

both as to the feasibility of a mission on the western
coast of Africa, and as to the spot most suitable for its
commencement. For this purpose the Rev. John
Clarke, of Jericho, Jamaica, and Dr. G. K. Prince, who
had practised the healing art there with reputation and
success, were invited by the Committee to proceed on
this necessary errand. Their long residence in the
tropics, and their knowledge of the negro character,
gave them special fitness for the work of exploration.
They embarked on board a trading vessel proceeding to
Africa on the 13th October, 1840, and after sailing
leisurely along the western coast, calling at Cape
Palmas and Cape Coast Castle on the way, they reached
the island of Fernando Po on the following New Year's
Day. Every opportunity of procuring information was
eagerly embraced. Intercourse with the natives was
everywhere sought, and minute inquiries were made as
to the probable reception of the messengers of the Cross.
At Clarence, Fernando Po, many of the inhabitants
were found to possess some acquaintance with English;
while from the situation of the island, nearly opposite
the important river Cameroons, ready access could be
had to the interior of the continent, which lay only
twenty miles away, presenting a coast-line of mountain and valley unrivalled for grandeur and salubrity
on the sea-board of the western coast. From Clarence
the travellers passed over to the mainland, visited the
chiefs, and met everywhere with a cordial welcome.
They, therefore, resolved, while awaiting the resolution
of the Committee on their report, to commence their
labours in Fernando Po, and to watch for the open-
ings that Providence might offer to the great region
beyond.

On reference to a map, it will be seen that Fernando Po lies in the Gulf of Biafra, near to the coast of Guinea. The island is about forty miles in length by twenty in breadth. It is nearly 120 miles in circumference, and, like the adjacent part of the mainland, is very mountainous; Clarence Peak, the most elevated point, attaining the height of 10,700 feet. The southern extremity is intersected by several steep mountains, varying from 1,900 to 3,000 feet in height, which, with the intervening valleys, are covered with dense forests of large and valuable timber, and watered by numerous rivulets. The wet season commences at the latter end of May, and continues till the end of November. The sea breeze is regular, but the land breeze is often intercepted by the high range of mountains on the mainland.

Clarence, the principal settlement, is on the north side of the island, in latitude 3° 53′ N., and longitude 7° 40′ E., and is built close to the sea upon an elevated plain, embracing two small peninsulas, Point William and Point Adelaide, with a semi-circular space extending about a mile in length, and forming a cove well adapted for shipping. The spot is fertile, and the water of the best quality. The tribes inhabiting the interior were in a state of nature—wild, savage, and without culture. But the people of Clarence were, for the most part, liberated slaves, brought there by the British cruisers, finding a sufficient livelihood in supplying the wants of the vessels frequenting the coast.

The labour of the missionaries among these people soon met with an abundant reward. By the beginning of the year 1842 five persons had been baptized, numerous inquirers gathered into a catechumen class, and a school of seventy children formed. The wild Adeeyahs of the mountainous interior had been visited, and the foundations laid for future labour amongst them. So encouraging were the reports sent home, that the Committee lost no time in announcing their decision, and in sending out the Rev. Thos. Sturgion and his wife, permanently to occupy the fertile field that the Island of Fernando Po seemed to present.

Now that forty years have elapsed since the resolution was taken to establish the mission on the West Coast of Africa, it may be useful to recall the objections and prejudices which had to be overcome. The resolutions of the general meeting of the Society open with the remark, that the obstacles to such an enterprise had hitherto been deemed insuperable. The inquiries of the deputation, however, removed this objection. But there were excellent persons who thought that the attempt to preach the Gospel to the children of Ham was a profane interference with a Divine decree. The African natives, they said, were suffering from "the judicial sentence of God against them;" but, affirms the resolution in reply, "the Gospel which repeals every national malediction, and addresses itself to every creature," had rendered this sentence of none effect. The asserted mental inferiority of the negro race was next dealt with; this, if true, it was replied, had doubtless been intensified, if not caused, by the horrid cruelties of slavery, and by the demoralising vices that it encouraged. But slavery, and the slave trade, had received an irrecoverable blow by the action of the British Parliament, and missionary culture elsewhere sufficiently proved that the negro mind was fully capable of instruction. With regard to the deadly nature of the climate, it was hoped that its perils might, in great mea-

sure, be overcome by the employment of men acclima-
tised in the tropical regions of the West Indies, and
fitted, by natural constitution, to encounter its dangers.
The agency offered by the Jamaica churches would, it
was thought, meet the difficulty, and the new army of
the Lord could be officered by a few trained men that
England would supply. Thus the churches of Britain
might fitly celebrate the fiftieth year of the Society's
existence, and hope to find, even in Africa, "a place
for the Lord, a habitation for the mighty God of
Jacob." "No field," adds the committee, "is more
worthy of cultivation than this, nor is any more likely
to repay the toils of the husbandman."*

In order to facilitate the proposed arrangements, Mr.
Clarke and Dr. Prince early in the year (1842) took
ship to return to England. By a "signal providence"
their vessel, struck by lightning and dismasted, was left
to the kindly influences of the trade winds, and drifted
across the Atlantic to the West Indies. Some days
were spent among the Windward islands, but at length
the voyagers reached Jamaica. Their unexpected
coming aroused the enthusiasm and touched the sym-
pathies of the congregations. The hand of the Lord was
in it. Numerous candidates for service in Africa came
forward, some of whom were examined and approved.
The stay of the two explorers, however, was brief, and,
again taking ship, in company with the Rev. Joseph
Merrick, who resigned the charge of a large church at
Jericho for the mission work, the voyagers reached
England on the 8th September. Their presence in
numerous meetings served to deepen the interest of

---

* Report for 1842, resolutions of the fiftieth annual meeting.

British Christians in the evangelisation of Africa, and, in the course of a few months, the services of four brethren, with their wives, were accepted. One of the four was Alfred Saker.

For the transport of the West Indian contingent, a sailing vessel, the *Chilmark*, of only 179 tons measurement, was engaged. It was resolved, that Mr. Clarke and Mr. Saker, with their families, should proceed in her to Jamaica, and accompany the chosen band. The rest of the missionaries, led by Dr. Prince, sailed direct for Fernando Po.

The sorrows of parting with many beloved friends, both in Kent and in Devonshire, were deeply felt by Mr. and Mrs. Saker; but on the 16th August, 1843, the last words were spoken, and, with their little daughter Eliza, they left London for Portsea, there to embark. The same evening a farewell service was held in the chapel of the Rev. C. Room, in which Mr. Saker, with his companions Mr. Clarke and Mr. Hume (a Baptist missionary, likewise bound for Jamaica), took part. The ship did not arrive at Portsmouth till the 18th. Early on the 19th they went on board the *Chilmark*, and by ten o'clock were passing through the Solent. "We had," says Mr. Saker, "a lovely view of the garden of England, the Isle of Wight. Its glens, hills, parks, and towns appeared in beauteous prospect. Towards night we passed The Needles, and ere morning anchored at Poole." The voyage commenced auspiciously; but in a day or two the weather changed, baffling winds hindered their progress, calms delayed them, and sea-sickness afflicted all the party. The smallness of the vessel, the scanty accommodation provided by the owners of the vessel, and bad provisions added to their misery. Mr. Saker was compelled to sleep on the floor of the saloon, and the eight weeks that the voyage to Jamaica lasted were passed in great discomfort, and ofttimes distress. Still the days were utilised by much reading. An Adeeyah vocabulary prepared by Mr. Clarke was copied, and the elements of the Houssa grammar were studied. In his remarks on their pursuits, Mr. Saker, in his diary, thus early betrays the purpose he had formed :—"May the Lord assist me," he says, " to study these languages until we shall be able to give to the millions of Africa the word of God in their own tongue." The Sabbaths too were days of delight, and, in holy worship of the Master they served, the little band found consolation and peace.

On the forty-eighth day of the voyage, at dawn, the welcome cry was heard of "land ahead." "After giving utterance to my grateful feelings," says Mr. Saker, "I hastened on deck to see the long-desired object. The head-land of Deseda was clearly descried in the distant gloom. I ascended the rigging, and, after half-an-hour's search, just caught a glimpse of the dark outline of Antigua, rising like three majestic rocks on the distant horizon. Oh ! it was a pleasant sight, after forty-eight days' imprisonment to the narrow limits of a vessel, and the monotonous scenes of a long passage." During the day Guadaloupe, and nearer at hand the romantic islands of Montserrat, Nevis, and St. Kitts, were passed; but contrary winds delayed their approach to Jamaica. On the afternoon of Friday, the 13th of October, the grand outlines of the Blue Mountains came in sight, to the great joy of the voyagers. The morning of the day was squally, and at midday thunder, lightning, and rain stayed their course. Some of the sails of the vessel were torn in pieces by the violence of the storm. The next day, Saturday, was calm, and before noon the ship was safely anchored in the harbour of Port Royal. In the evening the party was heartily welcomed by the brethren and friends in Kingston.

Mr. Saker conducted the services of the Lord's-day at Spanish Town, and returning on Monday to the *Chilmark*, sailed with his family to Black River, where they spent three weeks of grateful rest and enjoyment with the esteemed missionary, the Rev. Thos. May, whom they had known at Saltash, in Devonshire. Most gratifying visits were also paid to the venerable missionary, the Rev. Thos. Burchell, at Mount Carey, and to the home of the Rev. Thos. Cornford at Montego Bay, with whom also they had been previously acquainted in England; thence they proceeded to Falmouth to embark for Africa.

The six weeks thus spent were occupied by the brethren, aided by the pastors of the churches, in collecting the negro converts who were to assist in the mission, some as missionaries and others as settlers. In all, forty-two persons, including children, entered on the generous enterprise of civilising the savage tribes of Africa, and of giving to its perishing myriads the bread of life. The deepest interest was manifested by all classes. Valedictory services were held in every part of the island. The closing service took place on Tuesday evening, November 28th, when a crowded assembly gathered in the Baptist chapel in Falmouth, at which numerous addresses were delivered and much prayer was made. Fifteen hundred persons remained at the close to celebrate the dying love of the Saviour,

looking forward to the day when He shall come in
His kingdom, and gather all the redeemed from among
every people and nation to His feet.

At length the preparations were complete, and the
Chilmark sailed from Falmouth on the 1st December.
Writing the next day, the devoted Knibb said, "The
Chilmark sailed yesterday, and is now in sight of
Kettering. She carries a noble band of missionaries.
If ever I wished to have my likeness taken, it was
when I requested and obtained permission to steer her
out of harbour, which under the directions of the captain
I accomplished. Oh, it was an interesting, it was a
noble sight!"

Contrary winds, adverse currents, and calms delayed
the vessel for many days in sight of Jamaica. On the
11th she was still opposite the east end of the island,
and it was not till the 13th that the voyagers lost sight
of the "Queen of the Antilles." On the 22nd they
passed Watling's Island not expecting to see land
again until the Cape de Verde Islands should come
into view.

Mr. Saker cheerfully shared the labour of instructing
the various classes that were formed for the study of
subjects likely to be useful to the Jamaica brethren in
the work before them. Divine service was held every
day, as well as on Lord's-days, both in the cabins and
the steerage, where most of the emigrants were lodged.
The monotony of the passage was also dispelled by
light occupations and amusements, such as the weather
and the sea allowed. A voyage, however, that might
have been agreeable and profitable in every respect,
was often made miserable to all by the violence of the
captain, the drunkenness and blasphemies of the crew,

the scarcity and bad quality of the food, and the wretched accommodation provided for the passengers and their families. The captain set an example of rudeness, contempt, and injustice towards the coloured people, which the sailors were not slow to follow. The pain suffered by Mr. and Mrs. Saker from his harshness, amounting at times to inhumanity, was aggravated by anxiety on account of Mrs. Saker's delicate condition. In other respects the voyage was not without its intervals of pleasantness. After leaving the West Indies, favourable winds were enjoyed, and no very heavy storm was encountered. Harmony prevailed in the missionary band, and diligent advantage was taken of quiet hours to study the languages of Africa, and to prepare for the task that lay before them. On the whole, notwithstanding the crowded state of the ship, the health of the entire crew and passengers was good.

A few extracts from Mr. Saker's journal will suffice to indicate the character of the voyage :—

"*December* 13th.—A favourable wind sprang up during the night, which, by the morning, at eight o'clock, carried us out to sea, so that we lost sight of the Blue Mountains. Very thankful to get away, after so many days of vain effort against the wind. The distance from Falmouth to the east end of Jamaica is not more than fifty miles ; yet it has taken us twelve days to make it, and we hoped to get through the Windward passage in eight days. Toward evening St. Domingo came in sight, and we have hope of passing the island soon."

"*December* 16th.—About noon a vessel was discovered bearing on our course ; the wind being very light, she made but little progress. Towards sunsetting she

2

approached sufficiently near to show the number, when
we distinctly read, *Hopewell.* Intense was the feeling
of all on board, as the vessel came near, to speak; ' Was
all well?' 'Have you anything from England?' A
pleasant interchange of question and answer followed;
but night had so far advanced that the vessel was only
distinguished by her lights. On separating, we burnt a
blue light, and sang, 'Jesus shall reign where'er the
sun,' &c. In return our friends gave three cheers. I
sent off two rockets. We closed the day in public
prayer on deck. The vessel had on board Mrs. Knibb
and child, Mr. Dutton, Mr. and Mrs. Abbot, missionary
friends bound for Jamaica."

"*17th, Sabbath Day.*—I have preached to-day on the
authority of Scripture from 2 Peter i. 16. The seamen
seemed much impressed. Mr. Clarke preached in the
evening from Genesis xv. 1."

"*December* 22nd.—Yesterday we passed Inagua, a
low barren island, and we have to-day left behind us
Acklin's and Crooked Islands, thus bringing us once
more on the bosom of the mighty Atlantic. We have
safely passed the dangers of the Windward passage.
We are all in health, and peace reigns among our little
band, though they have cause to complain. The captain
annoys us in every possible manner."

"*December* 27th.—A good wind and straight course.
Much seaweed and many fish. My dear wife and child
continue well. May my heart rise in gratitude for such
favours."

Glad indeed were the voyagers when the mountains
of Fernando Po came in sight on the 15th February. But
a calm delayed their approach, and was the forerunner
of a fearful tornado, that threatened them with destruc-

tion, when just at their "desired haven." Through the goodness of God the storm passed away, and a gentle breeze bore them into Clarence Cove, where, about noon, they dropped anchor. Mr. Merrick and Mr. Christian met them on the shore, and gave them a warm welcome to the sphere of their future toil. "In the enjoyment of untold mercies, after a passage of eleven weeks, we are privileged," says Mr. Saker, writing to Mr. Angus on the 20th February, 1844, "to tread these shores, and mingle with the dear brethren here in thanksgiving and prayer. You, my dear Sir, and the thousands of British friends, who have offered up earnest, fervent, constant prayer for us, will know how to appreciate these tokens of Divine love, and unite with us in gratitude to God. They seem to me as evidences of His favour, cheering us in the mighty work in which our hearts are engaged, and saying, 'My word shall not return unto Me void,' and bidding us look with sanguine hope, yea, pious assurance, of a great and glorious success."

Such was the buoyant spirit and bright expectation with which Mr. Saker entered on the arduous career now opened before him.

CHAPTER III.

ON landing, the voyagers found that Mr. Sturgion and Dr. Prince were on a visit to the interior; but they hastened home on receiving a message from Clarence announcing the *Chilmark's* arrival. Dr. Prince and his party had reached the island in the previous September. They now gave the new comers a most affectionate reception. "We have been received here," writes Mr. Saker, "with every demonstration of joy which the friends could show, in a way suitable to the occasion, agreeable to our wishes, and honourable to the Gospel. We landed about noon on Friday, the 16th February, 1844. Before night every arrangement was made for the present location of all our company. The friends have cheerfully offered their homes to receive us, and supply us, according to their ability, with pious pleasure. In the evening, at seven o'clock, we assembled at the mission-house for thanksgiving and prayer. It was cheering to our spirit to meet such a company, and hear their simple, touching, expressions before God. After a hymn of praise we united in those sweet lines of Doddridge—

> ' Look down, O Lord, with pitying eye,
>   And view the desolation round ;
> See what wide realms in darkness lie,
>   And hurl their idols to the ground.

ARRIVAL OF THE "CHILMARK" AT FERNANDO PO.

'Lord, let the Gospel trumpet blow,
  And call the nations from afar ;
Let all the isles their Saviour know,
  And earth's remotest ends draw near.'

Surely the poet must have stood on the shore of
Fernando Po, so expressive, so appropriate are these
lines. The welcome was heartfelt and joyous. On
Sabbath morning a large company assembled at six
o'clock, when I preached from John iii. 16.* In the
evening Mr. Clarke preached an interesting sermon,
which was listened to with much attention ; I hope
profit. But what a scene! A house crowded with
thoughtful, attentive, and now respectably clothed,
hearers, listening with joy to the words of 'this life.'
Who can forget that, three years since, they were all
given up to work all wickedness greedily; but now,
' What hath God wrought ?' To Him be all the praise.
The vessel is now leaving, and I only add, I feel it in
my heart to live and die for the delightful work. I
bless God that I am permitted to see and hear, and
work in this heavenly field."

Mr. Saker soon began to experience some of the trials
which the missionary in Africa has to bear. The wood-
ants invaded and destroyed the contents of his clothes
chest. A tornado tore off the thatch of his house and
deluged it and all its contents with rain. Four times
in twenty days he was laid down by fever. His labours
at the printing press were constantly hindered by the
want of some necessary material. But these trials were
cheerfully encountered. "Individually and in my

---

* It is interesting to note that, under this first sermon of Mr.
Saker's, Thomas Horton Johnson was converted, who afterwards
became a most useful fellow-worker and friend.

family," he says, " numerous mercies are daily accorded
to us by our heavenly Father—so numerous that I
cannot attempt an enumeration."   Of these, not the
least was the safe delivery of Mrs. Saker of a little girl,
on the 25th February, the expectation of which event
had been a source of great anxiety and suffering on
board the *Chilmark*.

The moments were too precious to be lost in merely
curious investigation of the strange scenes around
him.   " From my landing till now," he says, writing
a little later, " I have been constantly engaged in
what we may call the outworks of our enterprise."
For already Mr. Saker began to display that remarkable eagerness for " work " which characterised him
to the close of life.   To the remonstrances of his
brethren that he was " doing too much "—" Too much
exposure, brother, will not do,"—his only response was,
" *Their* kindness in this respect I feel, and am desirous
of doing all I can to preserve the precious boon given
to us—health.   I know that European life is valuable
here ; but I must work while I have life, and I hope
the Lord will bless our efforts."

The accommodation provided for his family was
necessarily of the rudest kind, and much time was
occupied in making provision for it.   From the first,
Mr. Saker's skill as an artisan was put into requisition,
and building and furniture of every kind were
constructed under his direction, as well as by his
own personal toil.   " I have no less than five houses
building for the missionaries and teachers," he says, a
few weeks after his arrival, " besides my teaching, which
I have daily to attend to."   As the year wore on
severer sorrows came to him, fever frequently laid him

prostrate ; Mrs. Saker also was often ill, and their
new-born babe was taken from them to the enjoyment
of an immortal life. On the 31st July he writes to the
Secretary of the Society :—

"We have still to enumerate afflictions and mercies.
I would rather leave out the former, but I must tell
you briefly. I recovered very slowly from my late
attack of dysentery, and it was not till last Monday I
felt able to assist brother Merrick in attempting to cast
some quadrates for the printing-office. Such was the
deficiency that we felt we must wait a supply from you,
unless I could succeed. Impelled by such consideration, I made my moulds from some old lead, and
borrowed a ladle. Thus equipped, I set about casting,
and by Wednesday noon had finished nearly a thousand,
quite to my satisfaction, and the joy of my dear
brother. But the labour was too much for me, and, ere
I had accomplished all I wished, my strength failed, and
four hours of fever every night since still keeps me low.
Sabbath-day a fit of vomiting of four hours laid me
prostrate, and I feel exceedingly weak now. Still the
Lord is gracious to us."

"Since my dear wife's fever, the infant babe has
passed through much suffering; but now those sufferings are closed for ever. Parental feelings have been
stretched on this severe loss; but all is well. We
would not call her back again to earth. Yes, dear
brother, while prostrate on the bed through weakness,
and maternal tenderness watching and nursing the
suffering one, her spirit fled ! Before our Sabbath lamp
had ceased to burn, she fled to the glorious regions of
light and joy, to enjoy an eternal Sabbath of happiness
with the adorable Redeemer."

" On Monday, brethren Clarke, Prince, and Merrick came to confer on a place of interment. This was soon decided, and at 12 o'clock a lovely spot in the Mission House garden was consecrated by the reception of this innocent, this first of the Mission families that has fallen here."

Other trials could be more lightly borne. At the close of the year he tells us that all the missionaries were suffering from destitution of some of the necessaries and many of the conveniences of life. "No biscuit, no flour, no sugar, no butter, no meat of any kind, except sometimes a fowl, a squirrel, or piece of good mutton. Yam, our chief dependence, is now getting scarce. But I do not complain. The host of self-denying men in ancient and modern days would at once reprove my carnal heart. Oh! for the zeal of an apostle, to spend my days in cheerful labour to spread the knowledge of the great salvation!" It was enough for Alfred Saker to be engaged at any cost in any department of this noble task. To promote the kingdom of righteousness and peace he desired to labour night and day; for this end he wished to live, and in this work to die.

Early in the year (1845) Mr. Saker paid a visit to Mr. Merrick at Bimbia, and with him traversed several of the neighbouring towns. While thus engaged fever again assailed him, and by the advice of Dr. Prince, who hurried from Clarence to his help, Mr. Saker returned thither. The arrival of the *Dove* from England on the 22nd March, with her band of new missionaries, the Thompsons and Newbegins, and Miss Vitou, not only relieved the many pressing wants of the missionaries, but enabled Mr. Saker to commence the achievement of a desire he had from the first cherished, —that of opening a new station on the Cameroons river. When first built, the *Dove* was intended to sail as a steamer, and her engines and machinery were to have been placed in the charge of Mr. Saker. But certain defects in her construction led to her being employed as a sailing vessel only, and thus Mr. Saker became free to enter on the sole duties of the missionary life. He says, "I cannot express the high satisfaction I feel when looking at the *Dove;* I have not been without my dis-appointment at the 'minus engines,' but I am sure that all is well. It will not be possible to ascend any one of the rivers without a 'power' superior in strength to the current, and it will be equally futile to attempt it before our hands are strengthened by aid from home. We need fifty brethren now for the great work. If the Lord has need He will soon send them. May we be strengthened to persevere. The gentleness of the *Dove* seems to destroy the thought of the sufferings we have endured for the want of it; and I am confident that God will bless His servants in the use of it to His glory. Soon, soon may its wings be stretched, till all the nations far and near be converted to the heavenly Kingdom of Jesus and His Spirit."

In the month of April a brief visit, chiefly for health, was paid by Mr. and Mrs. Saker, in company with Dr. Prince, to a district already marked out, about twenty miles up the broad estuary of the Cameroons, as suit-able for a missionary station.

After passing the mangrove swamps which lie on both sides of the river's mouth, and whose poisonous reaches are pierced by many tortuous channels leading to the interior, the eastern shore changes its character, and from the sandy beach begin to rise low cliffs of rich red-brown earth, generally covered to the base with various shrubs and trees, interspersed at the top with cocoa and oil nut-palms. The first native settlement that is reached is the town of King Bell, and is marked by the canoes and traders' sheds that line the river's brink. Beyond this another beach, with its numerous canoes, points out the landing place of a still larger town, the residence of the chief, King A'kwa, the head of the most powerful of the tribes on the river. A little farther on, and on the same side of the stream, is situated Dido Town, lately founded by a branch of the A'kwa family. The chief occupation of the people is the collection of palm-oil and ivory from the natives of the interior, with which they barter with the traders, whose store-hulks lie off the town, for the cloth and tobacco, the beads and trinkets, that form the bulk of their trade.

Assured of a welcome by the chiefs, Mr. Saker, on his return to Clarence, at once made preparation to occupy one or other of these native settlements as his permanent residence.

The *Dove* being otherwise employed, Mr. Saker engaged a small schooner, the *Wasp*, and with Horton Johnson, on the 10th June, proceeded to commence his work in the Cameroons river. In thirty hours they reached King A'kwa's town. The next day they landed a portion of their boxes at Dido Town, taking a house offered them by the chief on their former visit. At this King A'kwa was indignant. Was he not king? Was not Dido his inferior? He was old, too, and would not live long. So he sent to demand the immediate surrender of the missionary. As Chief Dido replied

with defiance, the war-canoes were ordered out, and
next morning it seemed as if a furious onslaught on
Dido Town would alone avenge the injured honour of
the King. Mr. Saker, however, immediately interposed.
A palaver ensued, and, after twenty-four hours' negotia-
tion, the King triumphantly bore away the missionaries
with all their belongings.

The house hired of King A'kwa was built of wood, and
consisted of one room only—twenty-one feet by fifteen.
It had been erected a few months before by a trader
for the King's own use. Here, on the 16th June, 1845,
Mr. Saker, with his companion, took up his abode, and
began his ministry as a messenger of Christ to the
Duallas. A few extracts from his letter to Mr. Angus
will best describe his first movements :—

"*Tuesday*, 17*th*.—Slight fever, and much weakness
all day."

"*Wednesday*, 18*th*.—Much better, rested all day.
Dreadful storm at night, the rain breaking in so as to
cover the floor."

"19*th* and 20*th*.—Much better. Began the addition
of two rooms to the present, in hopes of being complete
before my family arrives. These rooms will be constructed by the natives, and made of the same material
as their own huts—bamboo mats and rods."

"21*st*.—Sat nearly all day at the language with interpreter. Enjoyed much communion with God. One
of my happiest seasons in prayer this morning. Felt
much enlargement of heart when praying for the
heathen, my brethren, and the Society. I am constrained to say, ' O Lord, renew the visits of Thy love.' "

"*Sabbath Day*, 22*nd*.—Rose early and met the chiefs
and people of A'kwa town soon after six. We had a

good meeting, and they sat patiently (nearly two hours) to hear the word of God. At nine the children with a few adults came to our little house. Johnson and myself sat with different companies till twelve o'clock. At half-past twelve I went to King Bell's town to have my first meeting. Was a little disappointed; could not collect more than about twelve, who sat with the king for about half-an-hour. I tried to engage their attention, but they had drunk too much, so I left them, and walked on to Joss's town. After waiting a little we had a large but noisy company. I do hope God will answer the many prayers of His people on their behalf.

"After returning and refreshment, we visited a town lying back in the bush between A'kwa's and Bell's town. Here we had a meeting which I think I shall never forget. As I explained the design of Christ's mission into our world, and illustrated His Divine power by His miracles, and His love by His freely giving Himself to death for us, the astonishment and manifested surprise of these people is past my power of utterance. About 105, old and young, sat in a circle before me, with an attention surpassed by no congregation at home. To me it was an hour of hallowed feeling. We left with fervent prayer that God would bless His word, fulfil His promise, and make the heathen His own."

Thus passed the first week of the laborious life that Mr. Saker now commenced among the tribes of the Cameroons.

On the 28th Mrs. Saker with her little daughter arrived in the *Dove*, in company with Miss Stewart, Mr. Clarke, and Mr. Merrick.

A VILLAGE ON THE CAMEROONS.

CHAPTER IV.

Perils among the Heathen, 1845—1846.

R. SAKER was now fairly launched on his life's work. He was surrounded by a multitude of heathens, without a head or leader, for with King A'kwa's mortal illness his authority was set at naught. Every one did that which suited his disposition best, under no control, and delighting in cruelty and revenge. The better informed among the people were traders, and a few of them were thoughtful and serious. These endeavoured to maintain some degree of order. They showed Mr. Saker and his family much kindness, and, what in his estimation was far better, they were desirous to hear the Word. They did all they could to protect the missionaries and their property from the hands of violence. "I cannot," said Mr. Saker some years afterwards, "describe to you the condition in which I found this whole people. A book they had not seen; the commonest implements of husbandry and tools of all kinds were unknown. I brought with me tools to make my own dwelling. My circumstances were for a long time on a level with the natives'; our food was nearly the same, but we were clothed and they were not."

The station Mr. Saker formed at King A'kwa's town, and which he now named Bethel—the house of God—

is situated about twenty miles from the sea, on a high
bluff on the eastern or left bank of the river Cameroons,
which disembogues its waters about four degrees north
of the Equator, nearly opposite the northern end of the
island of Fernando Po. The space of about a mile
separates the town of King Bell from that of King
A'kwa. The territories of the two chiefs are conter-
minous for some distance into the interior, and, as a
consequence, the two tribes were often at variance and
war. Although the river somewhat winds in its course
to the sea, the sea-breezes have almost direct access to
these two towns, and, being clear of the dense mangrove
swamps which line the sea-shore and spread on either
side of the river's mouth, the mission premises on the
Cameroons are more healthy than Bimbia and other
spots on the coast. The cottages of the people lie along
the river and spread for some distance inland, shrouded
by trees and bananas, the paths encumbered by bush.
The food plantations of the natives are still farther
inland, and are cultivated almost entirely by the wives
of the people, of whom the chiefs have many and the
ranks below them as they can afford to buy.

Higher on the same side of the river is Dido town,
and farther still is John A'kwa's town, the chiefs of
which recognise King A'kwa as their superior lord.
These towns are a mile or two apart. Crossing the
river obliquely from John A'kwa's town, but higher up,
we come to Preso Bell's town, or Hickory, inhabited by
a branch of the family of King Bell. The river here is
about a mile broad. All the tribes dwelling in these
towns speak the Dualla language. At the time the
mission began they were in a state of unfriendliness, if
not actual warfare.

KING A'KWA'S HOUSE AND STREET.

They were, in fact, utterly barbarous, practising the wildest and most debasing superstitions, and given up to the practice of every vice that degrades humanity. The work to be accomplished, and the condition of these savage tribes, can only be understood by a few illustrations. One day, on visiting Bell Town, the missionaries passed by the side of the river a corpse lying unburied, and mangled by dogs. It was the body of a man from Wuri, drowned by the upset of a canoe. No persuasion could induce the king to order its interment. Their entreaties were laughed at. " The man," said they, " is not a Dualla man." Another day the brethren were shocked to learn that the chief, Dido, had cruelly killed one of his wives and a slave. Another slave was thrown into the river, bound ; but, getting loose, he swam ashore, and fled into the bush.

Mrs. Saker mentions the following instance of barbarity :—

"One of our first converts, a woman called Anna, was on the way to chapel one Sabbath morning. On passing the Egbo house (where the men practise their superstitious rites), she heard the cries of women. On pushing the door open, she saw two women hanging by their wrists from the roof of the house, and being rubbed all over with a kind of herb that produces a fearful irritation. The cries of the poor creatures were most distressing. Anna begged they would untie them. They instantly seized her, and tied her in the same way, rubbing the same herb on her. We did not hear of it for nearly six hours. Some of our young men, with Mr. H. Johnson, immediately went to the rescue. They had to fight their way in, but at length succeeded in bringing Anna away. She had been one of our brightest women, but from that day she was an idiot."

Nothing among these people is more fatal than a charge of witchcraft; one that is often made on the occurrence of any accident or natural death. A slave of King A'kwa's was thus accused. To try the truth of the accusation, she was first tested with poison. She was made to drink an infusion of a poisonous nut; but, although she speedily vomited the poison, which is usually regarded as a sign of innocence, she was tied hands and feet, and cast into the river. Another slave was savagely mutilated by her enraged master, and left in a miserable condition to perish.

Soon after Mr. Saker's arrival, in the month of July, King A'kwa died. Mr. Saker was at the time busily employed in making the doors and shutters of his new apartments. With a few boards and joists, and a little contrivance, by the end of August the walls of the new structure were finished, and the two rooms floored. But, on the death of A'kwa, indescribable scenes of disorder, confusion, and wrong ensued. The two elder brothers quarrelled and intrigued for the succession. The houses of the dead chief were ransacked. Even the box (or coffin) containing his remains was broken open, and rifled of everything of value. His wives and slaves destroyed the dwelling that he had occupied. The town was given up to plunder. In October the mission premises were invaded; the knives, books, spoons, and table linen, and, worst of all, the flour, on which life itself depended, together with the goats and fowls, were carried off. These disorders and plunderings continued till December, when the elder son was declared king through the intervention of her Majesty's naval officers on the coast. A better state of things then began to prevail.

It was in the midst of these disputes that A'kwa's fifty sons, with the chiefs of the tribe, assembled at Mr. Saker's cottage to sell it to him, together with the plot of ground on which it stood. The price was soon settled, but the purchase was followed by incessant bickerings among the vendors respecting their shares, and constant attempts were made to force more cloth and goods from the buyer. Three days after the purchase was completed, a large body of A'kwa's sons and slaves collected together, armed with firebrands, guns, sticks, and swords, and with wild noise and shouting demanded possession of the house. Reasoning was in vain. One son, in his rage, with his axe split the door of the house into three pieces. Eight days after another assault took place, which brought on the serious illness of Mrs. Saker and her child. On this occasion, however, other chiefs interfered; a goat was offered in compensation for the injury done, and, although the sense of insecurity was not removed, the missionary and his family were kept in peace, finding their refuge and safety in the Lord their God.

His house-building accomplished, Mr. Saker next gave his attention to the language. Although a tolerably large vocabulary had by this time been secured, it was not till the end of the year that Mr. Saker felt himself able to read, write, and converse with some fluency in the Dualla tongue. "About January 1, 1846," he says, "I completed a draft of my first classbook, and, if I had had much confidence in it, should have sent it home at that time to be printed for the use of the Dualla schools. I have made the study of the language my special work, and although I cannot say much as to the advance which I have made, yet I hope it is something; and I hope more, that I shall live to translate the whole Bible into the Dualla tongue. With Divine assistance I have a settled purpose so to do, and I hope not to relinquish my work till it is done."

Later on we shall see how this noble purpose was achieved. Reviewing his first year's work in May, 1846, in a letter to his sister,* he says, "When I remember that twelve months since I did not understand anything about the language, that we had no house at Cameroons to contain us beyond the single room, that during the time we have been not less than two months absent on account of health, that while at labour often afflicted and hindered in a variety of ways; but that now we can look upon things around us, and know that we have a substantial store-house for boxes, barrels, and provisions, which has occupied me one month this year in erecting, and that now we are in health, better health than when we commenced the year, surely I ought to be grateful! If we cease to speak of His mercy, the stones and trees around would reprove us. May our hearts be ever alive to His mercy, and that mercy assist us to go on with our work, till we shall rejoice over sinners converted to God. This is the result for which we hope and pray, and it will be with unspeakable pleasure that we inform you of such success; but we need your prayers and the prayers of all our friends. You must not forget that nothing short of

---

* In which, however, he omits to notice a visit paid to the Bassa towns in the interior.

Divine power is sufficient to effect so great a change. If this is necessary in England, how much more so with the heathen tribes, whose character is so accurately drawn in the first chapter of Romans! Forget not that it is among such we live and labour, and cease not to pray for us, and the success of the Word among us."

CHAPTER V.

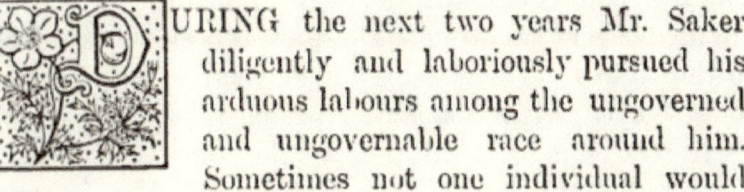URING the next two years Mr. Saker diligently and laboriously pursued his arduous labours among the ungoverned and ungovernable race around him. Sometimes not one individual would come to the worship, which was regularly maintained with the two or three assistants Mr. Saker had secured. Occasionally King A'kwa, with a few of his chiefs and attendants, would be present and give him a listless and uninterested attention. Or he would meet them at their frequent palavers, and endeavour to awaken their minds to some desire for the comforts and advantages of civilised life. A few children would fitfully attend the daily school, and repeat the little Dualla hymns and prayers their anxious teacher had prepared. Superstitious practices were employed to frighten him away. His path would be laid with the leaves of poisonous trees, with the hope that the touch of the missionary's foot would stimulate their fatal properties and destroy his life. From robbery the mission goods were never safe.

Besides these trials, necessarily incident to the work, others bore hardly upon the energies and spirit of the missionary and his little family. The pestilential climate would for days together lay him aside, while his beloved partner often sank beneath the fatigues, the privations, the anxieties, and the perils of their lot. The irregular communication with England frequently entailed severe suffering. There were no mail steamers in those days. Their stores failed, their supplies were long delayed, when some unexpected relief drew from their eyes tears of thankfulness, and from their hearts songs of grateful joy. In February, 1847, Mrs. Saker's health was so far impaired, and their little girl seemed so hopelessly ill, that the husband and father was constrained to send them to England. It was a bitter trial to be left alone in that land of " suffering, danger, and death." He feared, so ill were they, that they might never reach their native land, or that he himself might not live to welcome their return. His tender anxiety expressed itself in a letter to his wife, written on the 3rd April, to reach her soon after her arrival in England, when, among other words of affectionate thoughtfulness, he says, " I am very anxious to hear that all is well. How does the sea air and change of diet affect you ? Is there any sign of a return of last June's debility and danger ? Is there any change for the better ? Then the dear child! is the spleen reduced ? Is it still the same ? May we hope that she will live ? Ah! my dear H., let us mingle our prayers and trust in the Lord. For the present, farewell." Yet, a few days later, in the midst of all his afflictions, he could say, " Hope buoys my mind. I have many seasons in my solitude that words will not express. I have withal great reason for gratitude that I am kept so hopeful and quiet. My constant duties tend much to keep me in peace. If I had naught to do I should soon die with grief ; so that my earnest cry every day is for an energy of spirit, strength of body, and a heart devoted to the glory of God in the translation of the Scriptures and the publication of the Word of Life."

To a large extent the prayerful desire of his heart was fulfilled. Nothing could repress the ardour with which he pursued his toil. To his sister he writes:— " I rise every morning between four and five, and with brief intermissions for meals, &c., I am busy—the word is not expressive—I am more than busy; I am over-whelmed with cares and duties till eight, sometimes nine, at night; and what I am at this time most engaged in, I am trying my utmost to complete, the translation of the Gospels, and speedily, lest my health should fail before it is done. If my health fail again, I feel there will be no hope in any change short of Europe. And lest it should fail, I wish to have the work ready for the press, that it may be printed in England under my own care." .

Six months later, to the same correspondent, he says:—" During the day I have not time to sit down to eat bread, except a few minutes at nine, and again at five. I sit at my books, teach boys, labour with my tools. One day a carpenter, another a blacksmith, another a joiner, another a shipwright, or whatever is necessary. But my chief and all-important work at present is the study of the Dualla language, the pre-paration of elementary books, the translation of the Gospels, &c. This comes every day, and all other things, either as necessary repairs or needful occupa-tions, are attended to for recreation."

It is most interesting to note how this study of the Dualla language, and the preparation of a dictionary, grammar, Scriptures, and school-books are the theme of almost every letter. He cannot obtain the means of printing so soon as he desires, so he makes many shifts to supply the want. His invention, aided by his knowledge of iron work and engineering, enables him to cut a matrix, and to construct a rude press; but he is soon at a standstill for lead for the type, and he waits wearily for the chance of obtaining it from some passing ship. The books he needs are not at hand. "I wish," he writes to Mr. Angus, "some good-natured friend, who has the ability, could give me the volumes of the ' Penny Cyclopædia.' Do you know, my dear brother, I am sure I should be very thankful." Again, writing in January, 1848, to the Committee of the Society, he begs them to devote £10 or £15 of the surplus of his salary to the purchase of works on Biblical criticism, the Septuagint, and elementary works in Hebrew. "These books," he says, " I most want, and I beg of you, dear brethren, to let me want no longer. Look and see if you are not wrong in withholding books so long, and after repeated requests for them. Think of the position you have placed me in. In the midst of a heathen people—a people speaking their own language—a language I have been obliged to acquire. This heathen people I have to instruct, and open to them the way of life. But how shall I do this? I *must* read and explain the Word of Life in their own language, and I must translate that Word of Life, or how shall I succeed?" He then points out that his translation should be drawn from the Divine originals; but how can this be done, if he is not assisted by the solid learning of his predecessors in this task? Therefore, he pleads for the aid that learned works can supply; but,

while using every appliance within his reach, he, nevertheless, declares that he maintains "a constant, unwaver-
ing dependence on Divine aid." Anticipating the
objection that the early training of his youth could not
have fitted him for the achievement of the grand work
at which he aimed, he goes on to say that it was true
his early life was passed in occupations of another kind,
but he is now free to give his whole heart and mind to
the great task of Bible translation, and to make himself
competent for its execution; and, for the sake of this
" noble cause," he earnestly entreats the Committee to
grant him the requisite aid. That aid was not withheld, and in " due time " the devoted herald of the Cross
reaped the harvest of his desires.

But while the work of conversion was necessarily
slow among the tribes of the Cameroons, the Gospel
continued to make good progress at the seat of the
mission in Fernando Po. After the lamented decease
of Mr. Sturgion, on the 13th August, 1846,* the station
was placed in the charge of Dr. Prince, whose labours,
both as a medical man and a missionary, were of invaluable service in the early years of the Mission. In
December, 1847, Dr. Prince paid a brief visit to Mr.
Saker, at Cameroons, and at his urgent persuasion Mr.
Saker laid aside his studies for a short visit to Clarence,
the special inducement being the services intended for
observance on the baptism of several converts on New
Year's Day. Before leaving home he thus reports to

---

* Mr. Sturgion died of an illness contracted at Bimbia on a
visit to Mr. Merrick, in the month of July. He landed in Africa
on the 7th February, 1842, and was elected pastor of the Clarence
Mission Church on the 31st March, 1844. It then consisted of
forty-two members ; and of sixty-three at his decease.

Mr. Angus the progress of his labours: "You will receive a parcel by the *Rapid*, containing a few copies of our books. My Class Book, 1 and 2, is through the press. I have borrowed a page of type of brother Merrick, with which I have printed four pages, one page only at a time, of my Vocabulary, which extends to 400 pages of letter paper (4to) in manuscript, twelve pages of hymns, and twenty of Matthew's Gospel. These I use in the Dualla services, and hope in the beginning of the year to add the whole of Matthew, and increase my hymns to about a hundred. These will all be printed in the same size, page after page. But I hope the day is not distant when I shall receive a press and type, to enable me to print in a better manner. The whole of Matthew and Mark are waiting for the press; but printing in the way I have begun enables me to correct as I go on, and when complete a revised copy will be a proof sheet for an edition, whether it be printed in England or Africa. I shall be out of paper by the end of February, so must wait the supply which our brother Merrick expects."

The happiness and the rest were well earned which Mr. Saker now enjoyed at Clarence. He thus describes the scene of that New Year's Day morning:—" At six o'clock we all met at Waterfall. Three sides of a square were occupied by a devoted band of men and women, all in white. In the centre a desk. In the background a tent, and around the square not less than 200 inquirers and spectators. In front the flowing brook, winding in a delightful curve, and then seeking its way among the massive rocks, till at last it rushes over the precipitous fall. This, with the lovely bank, heavy foliage, and towering trees backing the stream, presented an enchanting scene. I read the 3rd of Matthew and prayed. Mr. Merrick preached from Philippians iii. 8, 'Yea, doubtless, and I count all things but loss for the excellency of the knowledge of Christ Jesus my Lord,' &c., &c. Dr. Prince then led nine candidates to the water side, and, after a solemn address, immersed them in the stream, in the name of the Father, the Son, and the Holy Spirit. This done, we sang another hymn, and returned to breakfast. But first, Dr. Prince and I walked through the town to see the sick, and it was ten when we ate our meal. At half-past three we began our missionary meeting, and it was a delightful happy meeting too. A collection was made amounting to £11. Yesterday morning I had to preach to the people. The text was a suitable one—" Grow in grace and in the knowledge of Jesus Christ, our Lord and Saviour." It was a very solemn sermon, and I felt the hallowing influence of the truth. I spoke with much freedom. At eleven I went into the school; a cheering sight: 260 scholars assembled, with not less than thirty teachers. At half-past three we met again for public service. Dr. Prince preached to a crowded house a baptismal sermon, argumentative and clear, and after an address to the newly baptized, he received them into the church, and we all communed together. At seven we dined, and spent the evening in cheerful song."

Refreshed by the fraternal and spiritual intercourse he had enjoyed, Mr. Saker, early in January, returned to Cameroons, visiting on the way the station of Bimbia, where, since his arrival in Africa, Mr. Merrick had laboured with great zeal and efficiency. In the few days of his sojourn with Mr. Merrick an incident happened which will well illustrate the evil customs of the people. A young man, while bathing, was seized by a shark, and in a few minutes his spine was torn out by the ravenous beast. Three men, two of them slaves, were accused of having bewitched the sufferer. They were seized, carried to the town, and put into chains. It was the Lord's-day, but after service Mr. Merrick and Mr. Saker went to the town and found a council sitting, consisting chiefly of slaves, debating with King William the doom of the accused men. The result was that, instead of being murdered on the spot, the trembling wretches were condemned to exile. One poor fellow was, however, allowed to accompany the missionaries to their settlement. A second escaped to the home of Mr. Christian, one of the Jamaica assistants ; it was soon surrounded by a violent crowd, and with difficulty the man was rescued. Ultimately he was sent away for safety to Clarence. The third man was not permitted to escape the doom intended for them all.

On reaching Bethel, the erection of a school-house at Bell's Town engaged Mr. Saker's attention, and another, to be used also for public worship, was begun at Bethel. The foundations of a house for Mr. Johnson, who had now resided with Mr. Saker fifteen months, were also laid. In these structures, progress was very slow, owing to the want of men who knew the use of tools. Then the mission-house itself was beginning to show signs of rapid decay. The wood of which it had been constructed was eaten into by ants, and threatened by its fall to entomb (African fashion) its inmates. This experience of the fragility of African structures gave Mr. Saker the greatest anxiety. Writing Mr. Angus, he says, "I do want to make myself a house as strong as the best wood and nails will admit, and I cannot patch up these mud walls many weeks longer. What to do I know not."

But, fired by zeal, and strengthened in his weakness by Divine grace, Mr. Saker pressed onward, cheered by the hope that ere long the light would dawn on the blinded eyes of the people around him. "Dualla is dark," he said; "grossly dark—dark as death; but, blessed be God, the Gospel which we bear is able to dispel it, dark as it may be."

CHAPTER VI.

ANXIOUS DAYS, 1848—1850.

IN the month of June, 1848, the general state of the mission constrained Mr. Saker, till relief should come, to take up his residence at Clarence. Of the band by which the mission had been commenced, only Dr. Prince, Mr. Merrick, and Mr. Saker remained. Mr. Sturgion and Mr. Thompson were dead. Mr. Clarke had returned to Jamaica with a party of the Jamaica immigrants, some of whom were driven from Africa by failure of health, and others were found, from various causes, unfit for the work. A few of them had died. Two or three only, men of tried courage and ability, remained. Dr. Newbegin's health had also broken down, and he had left for England. And now Dr. Prince and his wife were compelled by the deadly climate to hasten away, and to relinquish an enterprise in which they had borne so distinguished and useful a part. Writing to the Committee on the 5th July, Mr. Saker thus explains the reasons for his provisional settlement at Clarence : "In time past, we have had to mourn over the dead again and again. We have been called to bid adieu to the bereaved widow, and the afflicted wife and children. Our Jamaica band have almost disappeared, some by death—we hope now in glory—some by the disgraceful end of 'having loved this world.' In February, 1847, we were compelled to

part with afflicted sisters, one a wife [Mrs. Saker], and a dear child; in May, with Mr. Clarke and his sickly band; in September with brother Newbegin, and now a severer stroke has come in the removal of our beloved brother and sister, Dr. and Mrs. Prince. We have been weakened, chastened, and subdued, yet still our Heavenly Father removes not His hand. Sorrow comes on sorrow, and we are distressed. Oh, that we may ever bow with submissive love to all His will!"

"This *is* a trial! to send away those, the most useful, and without whom we know not how to go on, and we exclaim, What shall we do? This is the conclusion: Clarence is of more importance than Cameroons. Cameroons is less important than Bimbia. Then, Cameroons must be *laid aside.* I offer to take charge of Clarence till another shall relieve me. The doctor and his church thankfully accept it. It is decided, and I am your missionary resident at Clarence; and as to Cameroons, Johnson, aided by James Frazer at present, will do what he can while I am away." Under such circumstances, we cannot wonder at the bitter cry, the sorrowful moan which his loneliness forced from him in his letter to the Secretary, of the 14th June. "Oh! that our God may send us help speedily! Dear Sir,—Are the churches so destitute of young men, that labourers cannot be found for Africa? Are there none who can place their lives at the disposal of the Saviour in this sickly land? Do our pious youths forget that ours is a God *near and far off?* Oh! that the blessed Spirit may send you the men and the means, as well as the heart to send them here! We must have them speedily. Africa groans to be delivered from the bondage of sin."

Happily, in this sad state of things, Mr. Saker's health had gradually improved since the serious attack of illness that he passed through in the early months of the year. Aided by Miss Vitou, whose services in the schools were invaluable, he was able to meet the emergency, and with unconquerable energy to give every moment of time and every faculty of heart and mind to the duties that devolved upon him. The press he had with rapture received, through the liberality of friends at home, was set up in Clarence, and, with the help of some lads he had trained, he soon threw off many pages of school books and of Scripture for the use of the people at Cameroons. The services of the sanctuary in Clarence were usually crowded, both on the Sabbath and in the week. The prayer-meetings were filled with earnest worshippers, whose supplications for a Divine blessing on the Word received large and gracious answers from on high. Here is a sketch of his daily toil :—"I preach twice on Sabbath days, once in the week, attend the prayer-meeting on Tuesday evening, Monday evening being devoted to teachers' meeting, maternal meeting, and missionary meeting (in order). Wednesday evening, all the classes (and everybody connected with the church is in class) assemble in the chapel. Thursday evening a Bible-class meets at my house. Friday evening, public lecture. Saturday evening, to myself. Monday, Tuesday, and Wednesday mornings from ten to one o'clock, I instruct classes of inquirers (in which there are at present fifty). Monday evening, from five to six, another class who cannot attend earlier. My other hours are filled up in visiting the people, or in study, and even at my table I cannot sit without some one calling on some business." To

these constant and severe labours he added the superintendence of the "boys" whom he had taught to act as
compositors and pressmen, and the supply of manuscript
daily for the press. In his last letter of the year
(December 18th), it is no wonder that he should say to
the Secretary, "My legs fail, my knees tremble, and I
know not what I shall do. Yet, hitherto, I am mercifully
helped, and, with the exception of weakness in my
joints, my health is good. Pray for me, dear brother;
and send help as soon as you can."

But while Mr. Saker was thus toiling and writing,
the help he longed and prayed for was on the way. On
the 8th December the *Dove* once more left Gravesend,
having on board Captain and Mrs. Milbourne, Mr. and
Mrs. Newbegin, Mrs. Saker, and Mr. and Mrs. Yarnold,
the latter to assist as a teacher in Fernando Po. The
ship was also laden with a valuable printing press for
Bimbia, the gift of friends in Scotland and Norfolk; a
sugar mill, the gift of Mr. Peto; and with a large quantity of stores and provisions for the sorely tried workers.
By these arrivals the missionary band was increased
to eleven European agents (including the wives of the
missionaries), and eight native preachers and teachers.
A brief summary of the work accomplished in the
Mission up to this point is given in the Society's annual
reports. "Since 1841, the year of the opening of the
Mission, the bread-fruit tree, the pomegranate, the
mango, the avocado pear, and the mammee, fruits of
great value, and all suitable to the climate, have been
introduced by our brethren; garments sufficient to
clothe not less than 20,000 persons have been distributed; many hundreds of the natives, it may be said
thousands, have received medical assistance; three

principal stations (Clarence, Bimbia, Cameroons), have been established; and about eighty persons have been baptized. An 'Introduction to the Fernandian tongue' has been written by Mr. Clarke, and, with specimens of translation, has been published by him at Berwick. The gospel of Matthew, the book of Genesis, and Scripture extracts in Isubu have been published by Mr. Merrick at Bimbia; and Mr. Saker is engaged with the Dualla at Cameroons. Judging from these results, and comparing them with those of the first seven years of missionary labour in India, or other fields, we cannot but regard the labours of our brethren in Africa as very encouraging and important."

Anxious hearts, both on board the *Dove* and in Fernando Po, were awaiting the vessel's arrival, which took place on the 18th February, 1849. The voyage had its perils, for in the Bay of Biscay, on the 23rd December, she encountered a storm, which on the following day increased in violence, and continued to rage for several days. A sail was torn into shreds, the tiller was broken, the aft light was stove in, and the ship was nearly engulphed. The passengers, especially the females, suffered much from the incursions of the sea, as well as from the violence of the rain. At length, on the 6th January, they reached Madeira, and after refitting, proceeded on their way. The rest of the voyage though tedious, was pleasant. "It was Sabbath morning," writes Mrs. Saker, "at daylight, that we could trace land in the distance. No sea breeze until ten o'clock. But we were not seen by our friends on shore until one o'clock. I cannot describe how anxious I felt for many days before, but especially as we approached the island. I could not tell what lay before me; whether my dear

4

husband was living or dead, sick or in health." Not less anxious was the husband, who, for days, had been watching from the shore for the arrival of the "large mercy" for which he had longed and prayed. The Sabbath-school had just closed, when tidings came that the *Dove* was in sight. The fogs, called "smokes," which so often prevail on the coast at this season, had for many weeks been exceedingly heavy, so that any object three miles off could scarcely be discerned. A small glass gave evidence that something was approaching. "The news," says Mr. Saker, "fled through the town so quickly, that I had not time to prepare myself ere five or six of our people came up to tell me. Others ran to the beach to procure a boat, and soon a dozen friends were ready, seated in Mr. Lynslager's boat, to convey us to great joy, or heavy tidings. Rapidly the boat glided over the waves, and all doubt as to the identity of the vessel was removed; yet, no one was to be seen on deck, owing to the thick haze. We soon neared the *Dove*, and one by one I saw Captain Milbourne, brother Newbegin, a stranger, another, and another, but no Mrs. Saker. Another moment and a voice came pealing over the water, ' All right, brother.' A happy greeting followed. My dear wife had been obliged to go below from over-excitement. In a few minutes all our minds were calm, and, after reading the 103rd Psalm, we prostrated ourselves before God in adoring gratitude."

As the ship's dingy neared the shore, canoes and boats filled with people crowded about the new-comers; the whole town was moved, and every one, young and old, came out to show their welcome. Smiling and happy faces greeted them. After a slight repast, the bell sounded for worship, and a crowded assembly united in thanksgiving. Again, in the evening at seven, the church met to express in song and prayer the gratitude so strongly felt. Not less animating was the meeting held on the following day. It was a joyous gathering, for it spoke of hope and blessing for Africa; while it was an unspeakable relief to the heart of the burdened missionary. To use his own expressive words: "To me it has been an exhilarating time. It has had a happy effect on my spirit. But I feel unable to bear the joy, and I shall soon need a quiet, retired hour to moderate my feelings. The hour will soon come, for on Tuesday next the *Dove* will move on to Bimbia. Brother Newbegin and wife, Yarnold and wife, will take passage in her; and on its return it is probable I shall visit Cameroons with Mrs. Saker."

"The 18th February," he continues, "came, and was a day of joy. Our hearts beat more freely as we looked around on our brethren, blooming in health, and ready for the work. We hoped for large success." It was the expectation of Mr. Saker that the arrival of this band of helpers, radiant with health and hope, would set him free to return to Cameroons. But this desire soon received a check. Light sicknesses came as warnings of danger ahead. "Not to destroy hope," he said, "but they hindered labour, and became the precursors of heavier calamities." The first of these omens was the decision of Captain Milbourne to return to Europe. Then the health of Mr. Yarnold began to decline, and before the end of the year he felt constrained to abandon the work altogether. But the illness of Mr. Merrick, his departure from Africa, and death at sea in

the month of October,* was the most painful and fatal
blow of all. These distressing events compelled Mr.
Saker to reconsider his decision to return to Cameroons.
He ever thought of it as the true field of his missionary
labours. Not that his efforts at Clarence were without
reward. Many conversions testified to the power of his
ministry. The people were attached to him. His
medical knowledge added both to his influence and use-
fulness. An occasional visit to the Adeeyah tribes of
the interior encouraged him to make some efforts for
their benefit. His printing operations also went steadily
forward. But, under these circumstances, he felt it his
duty thus to write to the Committee: " I know the
mind of my brethren and the wish of the church. But
I do not feel willing to remain at Clarence. I shall, I
hope, yield to whatever may, in the judgment of the
Committee and brethren here, be my duty. The church
and the brethren write in one voice, and if the
Committee recommend it, I shall comply with the request of their letter. But my feelings are against it ;
my heart is at Cameroons."

But there was no alternative, and Clarence became
for a time the headquarters of his work. An occasional

---

* The Rev. Joseph Merrick was a native of Jamaica, and of
African descent. He was educated in the Society's schools, and
as a youth began in 1837 to preach. He was soon after associated with his father in the pastorate of the church at Jericho.
He entered on mission work in Africa in 1843, and laboured most
diligently among the Isubu tribe on the Bimbia river. He
quickly learned to speak their language with great readiness and
precision, and translated a portion of the New Testament into
the Isubu tongue. It was partially printed by himself, but was
completed at press by Mr. Saker. He died on the 22nd October,
1849, on his passage to England.

visit to Bethel was all that he could do. The voyage across the strait and up the Cameroons river was often perilous, often delayed for days together by baffling winds and currents. These he willingly encountered, frequently in an open boat, to assist and encourage the coloured brethren, Johnson and Fuller, whom he had left there. Under their industrious hands the seed Mr. Saker had sown began slowly to appear. He visited them in the month of April, and, writing to the Secretary a few days after his return, he says: "I heard from Johnson yesterday. The schools and meetings are still well attended. King Bell grieves his heart that I do not come back again. His entreaty is that I would send some one to teach his children. And, dear sir, what am I to do? At Cameroons, where I hoped to spend my days, they are not half provided for. Hundreds of children there are clinging around my heart, and I feel deeply distressed that I cannot go to them. What can be done? Entreat the Committee to let me have another native teacher."

Encountering a very stormy passage, another brief visit was paid to Bethel in the month of August, when Mr. Saker had the pleasure of marrying the first of the Duallas who submitted to that sacred and social rite. Three months after, the marriage was followed by the husband's baptism. To celebrate this joyful service, Mr. Saker left Clarence on Monday, the 5th November, having Mrs. Saker and Miss Vitou in company. At Bimbia they were joined by Dr. and Mrs. Newbegin. Tuesday and Wednesday passed in the endeavour to reach their destination in the face of a fearful tornado, and with disabled rigging, about six o'clock in the evening of the second day, they landed at Bethel. The fatigues

of the voyage could not repress his anxious desire to
gather in the first-fruits of his labours at King A'kwa's
town. "At eight o'clock," continues Mr. Saker, "we held
a prayer-meeting with our brethren, and a goodly company of Duallas. At four next morning we met a large
number of Duallas for prayer. This meeting continued till
six. On account of the tide we deferred our next service
till eleven o'clock, when we met again in the chapel.
Sang and read in Dualla. Mr. Newbegin then explained,.
through an interpreter, the chapter I had read, after
which I addressed the congregation in Dualla, showed
from the Scriptures the command of Jesus to disciple
all nations and then baptize them, and exhorted the
inquirers to a steadfast adherence to the words of our
Lord, and the path of righteousness. We closed with
singing and prayer, and then went down to the beach.
Another Dualla hymn was followed by an address to
the candidate. I then baptized this, our first convert,
in the waters of Cameroons. Oh, that this small beginning may be speedily succeeded by the ingathering of
a mighty host to the Lord our God! The spectators of
this (to them) novel scene were very attentive; silence
and order were observed by all. Deep seriousness and
anxiety were on the faces of many. Dr. Newbegin
closed with prayer."

The afternoon was devoted to the formation of a
church, consisting of Mr. and Mrs. Saker, Horton
Johnson and his wife, and Smith, the convert just
baptised. The services were closed by the celebration of
the Supper of the Lord. "Thus," concludes Mr. Saker,.
"I have lived to witness what I have long desired
intensely, the beginning of a good work at Cameroons,.
and the formation of a Christian church. Oh, that I

may see it increased to a thousand souls! And I
do hope, for the Spirit of God is doing a large work
there. More than twenty inquirers are hanging on
my heart and lips with marks of deepest solicitude.
The ferocious, demoniacal features are assuming the
softness of children, and those who a little time since
sought my life are saying to me, ' What shall I do to
be saved ?' I cannot describe my feelings when I see
and hear what I would record if I had but time. Dear
sir, pray for us, and rejoice with us too."

The regret of Mr. Saker that he could not himself
minister to these eager souls was the more intense,
because the chapel, built to hold 200 persons, was
now crowded with interested hearers, and that during
these visits hundreds more gathered to listen to the
words of grace which fell from his lips.

By this time, however, the tropical heats and fevers
were making their mark on the sinewy and spare
frame of Mr. Saker, and notwithstanding a run to the
river Gaboon in August, from which he returned
" much bettered," he yet felt it his duty to avail himself of the offer of a free passage, in the Mission vessel
of the United Presbyterian Church Mission at Calabar,
to make a brief visit to England. After seven years
of unceasing and exhausting toil, and many attacks of
illness, this change of climate was as necessary as it was
welcome. On the 12th of March, 1850, with his wife
and Miss Vitou, he left Clarence. The voyage was
tedious, but the tedium was more than compensated by
the improved health with which the party landed at
Liverpool on the ensuing 28th of May.

CHAPTER VII.

THE DAWN OF BRIGHTER DAYS, 1850—1852.

N Mr. Saker's arrival in England, he found that the condition of the African Mission had for some time occupied the anxious attention of the Committee of the Society. But scarcely was he landed when the necessity of immediate steps being taken for its re-inforcement was solemnly impressed upon them by the unexpected tidings of the decease of Dr. Newbegin, which took place shortly after Mr. Saker's departure from Clarence. This sorrowful event occurred near midnight, on the 17th April, at the mouth of the Calabar river, whither Dr. Newbegin had sailed in the *Dove* to obtain medical advice. Words cannot express the consternation with which the news was received. Not one of the English brethren sent out from England was left in Africa. The hearts of many of the sup-porters of the Mission failed.

It was at this moment of deep depression that Mr. Saker addressed the following remarkable letter to the Committee :—

" I have a fear that some of you who wish well to Africa will be discouraged, and I think you ought not to be. Let us review some of the facts. Ten years since you commenced the work. You sent many labourers and expended much treasure. Of those sent out, God has gathered to himself Thompson, Sturgion, A. Fuller, Merrick, and Newbegin. Prince and Clarke have been driven from the field, and a small company of West Indians have fled, terrified by the toil and suffering. This suffering and loss of life show that the sacrifice you have made is large. But ought we to have expected less? Bloodless victories are not common. Sometimes we have to wait long for the results we seek; but in this Mission God, in His Providence, permits us to look at something accomplished before this last affliction fell on us. Let me refer to these results. There are now living in Africa about one hundred souls hopefully converted to God. In nine years past, forty may have died leaving the pleasing testimony that they are gone to a better land. They are saved, instrumentally through you and your agents.

" There are now eight native teachers engaged, more or less, in efforts for the salvation of souls. They are not all supported by you, but they *are* what they *are* through you. The education imparted is an immense benefit. In the colony of Clarence you have effected a transformation unspeakably valuable, and almost unprecedented. Among the natives of this island, impressions have been made that only need fostering to result in the glorious and happy change you long to behold. On the continent it is difficult to say what has been done. Souls have been brought to God, churches formed, and actually the wilderness is now being transformed into the garden of the Lord.

" All this stands against so much suffering, and so many deaths; and will any say that the sacrifice equals the results?

" And we must not forget that all who die are self-devoted, and God has accepted this offering, and by it wrought all that we see accomplished.

" Brethren, I think you will feel with me, that we must not be discouraged. God afflicts us ; let us humble ourselves before Him, and try to bring to His service purer and more devoted sacrifices.

" You will doubtless conclude, that I ought to return to Africa immediately ; I can only say, I am ready."

This trumpet call to "Come up to the help of the Lord, against the mighty," roused every heart.

The history of the Mission was passed in review. The proofs of God's working in the conversion of souls by the preaching of the Word were patent, and destroyed every doubt in the minds of the Committee as to their duty. Fidelity to the great cause committed to their charge required the continuance of their efforts to win Africa for Christ. No past suffering, no prospective peril, could daunt the firm, calm resolve of Mr. and Mrs. Saker However fearful others might be, their lives were the Lord's, and to be spent in Africa for Him.

Arrangements for their return were made as speedily as possible, and on the 25th October they sailed from Liverpool. Owing to light winds and frequent calms, the passage was longer than had been anticipated ; but it was on the whole a pleasant one, and was crowned with a warm welcome, when, on the 29th December, on a Sabbath day, they entered Clarence Cove. "Truly," says Mr. Saker, " it was a day of joy to me and our people." Many wept for gladness, and within an hour and a half some five hundred persons gathered in the chapel, to rejoice in hymn and prayer that the Lord had not forsaken His heritage. The gratitude of the travellers was not a little increased by the fact they learnt on landing, that two vessels, in which they had endeavoured to secure a passage from England, had been wrecked on their way. Twelve days afterwards Mr. Saker was joined by the Rev. John Wheeler, who had been the pastor of the church in Windmill Street, Finsbury, London, and had nobly offered himself to share with him the perils of the Mission. He was immediately chosen to fill the office of pastor in the church at Clarence, and Mr. Saker was once more free to give himself to the work on the great continent so near.

Having set " in order the things wanting in the church " at Clarence, Mr. Saker paid a brief visit to Bimbia, where he collected the manuscripts and Isubu translations of the lamented Merrick. Leaving directions for their printing with Joseph Fuller, he hastened to Bethel, where he found a state of things that filled his heart with joy. He received " a truly Christian welcome," and became immediately busy with the examination of inquirers, and in listening to an account of the trials and persecutions through which the infant community had passed. Twenty persons were examined; fifteen belonged to the number of those who, in October, 1849, had given him reason to hope that a work of grace had been begun in their souls; but only five were for the present accepted for baptism; one, a slave; another, a prince belonging to a neighbouring tribe; and three females, each in years. " On Sabbath morning, the 2nd February, 1851," writes Mr. Saker, " we assembled at six o'clock in our chapel, which was soon filled. I read and explained to the multitude some of the Scriptures respecting the institution and design of baptism. I then addressed the candidates, and exhorted them to steadfastness. After prayer we left the chapel for the river. The candidates and a large company of inquirers followed me down the hill, while nearly 200 spectators took their station on the high bank overlooking us. We prayed again, and then baptized. Then it was proved that the Dualla is changed. Usually they express their joys and sorrows with heathen noise. Yet here was no noise, save the sobbing of those whose deep feelings could not otherwise be expressed. The tears rolled down many cheeks that day that have not been accustomed to weeping. Many said, ' Baptize me too.' We once more expressed our thankfulness to God, and then returned to the chapel yard, singing a sweet song as we ascended the hill. In the afternoon we received the newly baptized into our little church, rejoicing in these, and hopeful for yet greater numbers."

The converts had, through much tribulation, entered the kingdom of God. The congregation had been severely tried. The evident changes wrought by the Gospel stirred up the hatred of not a few enemies of the Cross, and efforts were made to prevent the access of the people to the chapel ; these failed, and at last the chiefs privately met to deliberate on the course to be pursued. It was resolved to destroy the mission station entirely, and to kill every native, male or female, who persisted in attending the ministrations of grace. A plan was secretly prepared ; but the principal chief was uneasy. To kill the young prince was certain to bring on a war with the tribe to which he belonged. Persuasion was therefore employed to detach him from Mr. Johnson. A special messenger was also despatched to Bimbia to fetch his sister, that her entreaties might be added to those of others. He listened, but declined to yield. In his turn, he spoke of Christ, and pleaded with her to forsake the world. One argument she urgently pressed. She said he would be killed, and in saying this revealed the plot that had been laid for the destruction of all who cleaved to the Word of the Lord. This at once opened his eyes to the danger; but he nobly replied: "Well, if they wish to destroy the Gospel, they cannot, and they shall not kill the missionaries till they have first killed me. We will die together. I now see why you are brought here. Go to the chiefs, and say to them, I will not leave the Gospel of God." The principal chief's heart failed. To kill the prince was perilous; so the word went forth : "Let the white men live." Still, many of the converts were put in chains and cruelly beaten. Twice Mr. Johnson rescued one woman from death. But at the time of Mr. Saker's arrival this season of trial had nearly passed away, and his heart was filled with joy " that God was making His own Word thus to grow."

It was not till the month of September that Mr. Saker was able to take up his abode again at Bethel, to begin, as he said, "a long and solemn work." For the few months during which Mr. Wheeler was passing through the fevers which usually attack a new-comer, Mr. Saker continued to assist him in the work of the church in Clarence. In April he visited the mountain people, and in June baptized nine persons below the well-known waterfall. Writing on the 28th August, he thus anticipates the labours before him at Bethel : "I now go to my loved work again. How soon I shall be able to write you from my deep mine of toil I cannot tell. Next week I must baptize many at Cameroons, marry some others, and then assemble all the children for examination and reward. Remember us in your daily supplications, and may the cheering presence of the Father of mercies be with you."

Almost his first task on arriving at Cameroons was to provide suitable dwellings for the Mission families. The frail and perishable character of the materials of which houses were usually built, and the destruction caused by the invasion of white ants, had early led Mr. Saker to devise some means for securing more durable structures. At first he tried the harder woods of the forests, but at length discovered that clay suitable for bricks and tiles existed on the spot. He first set up his brick-making shed and kiln at Clarence; but it was soon evident that the clay of Cameroons offered a far better material. Writing on the 3rd January, 1852, he reports: "I am happy to say that in this I have a complete success (both building brick and paving tiles), and for some weeks past my brickyard has been in active operation. I suppose that 10,000 are now ready, and we are making 2,000 a-week." The entire cost, he thought, would average about twenty shillings a thousand. To accomplish this great task he had himself to labour with his own hands, and to train the lads who were willing to submit to his tuition.

In a letter written a few days later, Mr. Saker enters into somewhat fuller detail of the way in which he attained his end. " In settling myself, seven years since, at Cameroons, I resolved to make bricks, if for no other purpose, yet for a good cottage for myself. For many months I tried, but in the end gave it up in despair. No persuasion or offer of payment would induce the men to labour. They laughed at us, and regarded us as slaves or fools. We could not get bricks, so built a chapel of wood, and the people filled it. They heard, and in time felt, the importance of preparing for the solemnities of another world. The truth made impressions on their hearts, and they were changed. Right principles began to have place, and when they went to trade in the country, they could no longer succeed by fraud or lies. As soon as this was seen, persecution came; and with the loss of all their property, and with personal suffering, they barely returned to tell their companions. And so it has happened that, as soon as a man decides for God, his own townsmen drive him from the markets, lest he should spoil their trade. In their sufferings they came to me to know what they were to do. I have replied, ' Cultivate more ground, raise and sell provisions, plant cotton, and open a new source of trade.' Latterly, I have said, ' *Make bricks and I will pay you.*' Now see the answer. ' We will do anything, if you will teach us?' I have taught them, and my brickyard maintains five families, and in return I get 2,000 bricks every week. This, my dear sir, is a triumph—a triumph which we owe to God, and the influence of His holy Word. *Without* the Gospel, I could get no work done; with it, I can build a bridge across our wide river, or convert the wilderness into a fruitful garden ; and, had I a sufficient sum of money to maintain a few families through two years of labour, I could open a new source of profit and dependence for our people. Even without money, I hope eventually to succeed in planting a few acres with cotton, even as we have with sugar cane."

But the possession of bricks was of little avail without mortar to cement them together. We, therefore, soon read : " In my travels, I am now searching high and low for a material with which to make lime or cement. I hope to succeed, and I purpose sending out my canoe to collect oyster-shells. If I can obtain sufficient, we shall soon have lime. And then, brethren, what can hinder our work? If the Lord gives me health, we shall do well." And he did well, for the Lord was with him. In a few years the mission-houses, the chapel, the school-houses, were all transformed, and they remain durable monuments of the practical knowledge, skill, and far-seeing sagacity of this wise worker in the kingdom of God. King A'kwa's town itself has changed its aspect. The brickmakers, the smiths, the carpenters, and the builders that Mr. Saker trained have in many instances exerted their newly-acquired skill in raising structures of brick, and improved habitable dwellings for themselves and others, instead of the frail bamboo and mud huts of their savage ancestors. Christianity and civilisation have gone hand in hand, scattering on every side the fruits and flowers of a higher and better life.

But Mr. Saker further describes for us, in his own striking way, the advances made in the evangelisation of the people:—

"A month since we baptized eleven more converts, and still we have several whom we approve. The congregation is numerous, and the devout attention to the Word by a large number is exceedingly pleasing. At four and five o'clock every morning the schoolroom is crowded to hear the Word of God, and in the evening the people will only retire when bidden. Numbers use every effort to learn to read. Many have succeeded; and then the joy, the astonishment, of their hearts at any fresh discovery of Divine Love as revealed in the

BETHEL CHAPEL, CAMEROONS.

Scriptures! They hold their lips, or beat their heads, as the expressions they read are explained to them, and are utterly unable to describe the emotions of their hearts. Sometimes they seem afraid to breathe, lest the wonderful idea should be disturbed and flit away from them; and they wait for minutes, unable to grasp the thought which comes upon them. The parables of Jesus are a continual feast for them. One thing may be recorded. Concern for instruction succeeds conversion; ignorance is not deplored till guilt is a burden. Our church now numbers twenty members; inquirers, twenty-five; a congregation which fills our little temple; school not large, but, I hope, efficient." He closes this deeply interesting narrative with the intimation that he had begun to attempt the same gracious work at the town of King Bell.

Scarcely, however, was Mr. Saker settled at Bethel than he was called away to Clarence, by the destruction of the chapel in a fearful tornado; and in the month of May the care of the entire Mission again fell into his hands, by the departure of his valued friend and colleague, Mr. Wheeler. It was hoped that a brief sojourn in England would enable Mr. Wheeler to return invigorated and restored, but this hope was disappointed. Mr. Wheeler failed to return, and for two years and a-half Mr. Saker was compelled to meet—alone and unassisted by any European—the many cares and anxieties of the entire Mission. But his indomitable courage never gave way. With his native helpers he laboured night and day. "In journeyings often, in perils of waters, in perils of robbers, in perils by the heathen, in perils in the wilderness, in perils in the sea, in weariness and painfulness," he pursued the great

5

object of his life, never happier than when, as the fruit of his self-sacrifice and zeal, he gathered a few sheep from the wilderness into the fold of God. Writing on the 28th of September, 1852, he says:—

" The work of Missions, *as we see it and feel it*, loses none of its interest. We have two scenes ever before us, and painted in unmistakeable colours. Here is wickedness in its most degraded and deadly form; misery, discord, and death float around us—a corrupting mass, a sea of death, subjects for deepest compassion, work for the purest benevolence.

" We have also a pleasant enclosure apart from this fearful scene; an enclosure where the voice of prayer and praise happily continue, where the lovely plants of a better clime are springing up and bearing fruit to God. All glory to Him who plants and waters the precious seed!

" In our churches we have enough to make us thankful in the steadfastness and piety of our members. That many endure so much and so well is a marvel. This is especially the case at Cameroons. That some are wavering, or worse, cannot be surprising. Since Mr. Wheeler left us we have buried four honourable members. The continued rainy season alone prevents us from baptizing some, and the number of inquirers is increasing."

" But there is one thing almost disheartening. We have three churches in as many different places. We have two other places where the Word is regularly preached; yet, what is the whole of this to the mass of men living in darkness around us? What proportion is a hundred members of churches to the tens of thousands treading the same soil, dancing before our eyes alike careless of God and themselves? What do we among so many? Where one regards the voice of mercy, thousands turn a deaf ear; and yet death goes on with his work; war, disease, and witchcraft are insatiable; and a generation is almost gone since I first saw this dreary land. This fearful woe is unmitigated, except we feel the value of one soul saved from ruin; and it is not of one only we rejoice; so our joy is great. Thus ours is a mingled lot—highest pleasure with disheartening sorrow. In such a land, what manner of men ought we to be?"

In another letter of this year he expresses regret that the cares which daily press upon him hinder his communicating the incidents that continually arise. How much could he say of the converts, of his assistants, of the condition of the people! What touching tales! What thrilling emotions their persecutions and deliverances excite! Then there are new converts, awakening hope and filling the heart with joy! "Then come the roarings of the adversary," for the "prey is taken from the mighty, and the enemy brings his host in the shape of a hundred slaves, armed with staves, guns, and swords, as on Monday last, surrounding the houses and threatening to drive us all away, and finally decamping with our cow and all the goods that can be seen. But all is useless. They see and feel that the cause is God's, superstition fails to hold them in chains as heretofore; and although Satan would excite them because their religion and the hope of their gain are going, yet, when left to think and remember all that they see and hear from us, their hearts fail, and thus, as last evening, they restore all that they took away on Monday. Such a thing was never known before. That an animal could

5*

live in their hands an hour is marvellous, especially
when hungry and excited to madness. But all things
—how can you know them if I fail to write? And yet
I could fill a very long sheet every week had I time or
determination equal to the task."

Indeed, but a small portion of Alfred Saker's life-
work can be described in the few pages allotted to this
biography. All that can be done is briefly to indicate
the nature of the toil, and the breadth of the labours,
which filled a life of unsparing devotion and relentless
self-sacrifice.

CHAPTER VIII.

THE MISSIONARY AT HIS WORK, 1853—1856.

HATEVER might be the difficulties and discouragements of the work, Mr. Saker found at Clarence and Cameroons abundant joy and gratification in the manifest growth of the kingdom of God, in its "righteousness, peace, and joy in the Holy Ghost." Not so among the Isubu people of Bimbia. This station was founded by the lamented Merrick on his arrival in Africa, and on a spot that was deemed the most healthy of any that could be found at the mouth of the Cameroons. A high promontory of basalt stands boldly out from the main land, breasting the waves of the Atlantic, and apparently free from the baleful miasma which ever lurks in the swamps and mangrove forests of the low-lying shores around. It has, however, proved to be the most deadly of any of the settlements on the coast, and every European missionary who has made it his residence, even for a temporary sojourn, has retired from it either sick unto death or smitten with malarial fever of long continuance.

For the first two or three years there were signs of progress, but it soon became manifest that the coming of the Gospel was too late to stem the torrent of iniquity and degradation that was hurrying the Isubu tribes to their destruction. The efforts of Dr. Newbegin, his successor,

were alike unavailing, and the wretchedness of the
population rapidly culminated in irrevocable decay.
Mr. Saker, too, found that the miseries occasioned by
internal discords, by the curse of witchcraft, by continual murders, by the unceasing wars with neighbouring tribes, were on the increase. As the natural consequence, the people were rapidly declining in numbers.
The means of existence were failing; the land ceased to
be cultivated; fishermen no longer plied their calling;
incessantly harassed with trials for witchcraft, they fled
to other spots. The endless fighting cut off the supply
of yams, maize, and plantains from the interior. If one
man toiled and planted to feed his family, his canoe was
burnt and his field and home were invaded until the
devastation was complete, and, to use the forcible
language of Mr. Saker, " hunger pined in every corner."
The few converts, though cared for by the missionary,
were in constant peril. This disastrous state of things
determined Mr. Saker to remove Mr. and Mrs. Fuller to
Cameroons, and with them the printing materials and
such of the remaining buildings as would be useful, and
to confine the mission to one native schoolmaster. His
own visits would for the future be of a purely evangelistic character. If any other consideration weighed
with him in coming to this decision, it was the unhealthy
character · of the place, which was constantly on the
increase from the growth of bush and swamp following
the decay of cultivation and the rooting out of the
population.

A short extract from a letter of Mr. Fuller (July,
1853) will vividly depict for us the horrors of the
savage life by which he was encompassed :—" In June,
on the third Sabbath day, the noise of drums was heard,

a canoe made its appearance at the point, and what was this noise? The drum was telling (the natives can make their drums speak) the horrible tale of their cruel deed. It was too awful a sight for me to witness; but those who saw it said that a man's head, newly cut off, was at the bow of the canoe. It was the head of a poor innocent creature taken by a man by name Ngganda, or Dick Bumbi, and for no just cause, but simply for what they call 'a hero.' This was soon followed by a grand festival, the particulars of which I am unable to give."

As there was no prospect of any reversal of this state of things, the Committee, in 1870, resolved to withdraw their single agent at Bimbia, and it has ceased to be occupied as a station. It is, however, occasionally visited by the missionaries in their passages to and from Victoria, and the knowledge of the "way of life" is not allowed utterly to die out in the land.

At Cameroons how different was the scene. Here substantial buildings were gradually springing up—a mission-house to last for years to come, and to be a fixed base for future operations, and a house which, when finished, would accommodate a family and all the visitors it might have to welcome. With it were a school-room, a printing office, a safe store, an artificer's shop, and a chapel, also lesser structures for printers and servants attached to the Mission. "Stand with me now, dear brother, a minute," says Mr. Saker, writing to the Secretary of the Society (November, 1854); "we are in the school-room, at present appropriated to printing. The press is just put up, the type is in cases, and here stands Fuller at my right hand. Next him is Songe; near him is Dikundu. At my left hand is Dumbe. Coming in at the door is N'kwe. Behind him is Carra. Excepting

Fuller, all these are native converts.* Few of them are preachers. Johnson is elsewhere at this minute repairing my boat, and with him a company of pious labouring lads. Those named are all young, from eleven to twenty-eight—young men of approved piety, full of zeal, only waiting a command to do anything, to bear the lamp of truth into the darkest dens. Here, to-day, they have each their employment; on the coming Sabbath they will be scattered, all at work."

Now let us pass from this graphic and interesting picture to another drawn by the same vivid pen: " It is evening. I am sick, but writing you. Fuller and Johnson both are near. They are examining candidates for baptism. This final examination is on Fuller's account, that he may know the value to be attached to profession, and be gladdened to trace the leadings of the Holy Spirit. And now they come in with a list of eight approved. Their names are read. I know them all, and on Sabbath they are to be baptized by Johnson, Fuller to preach. Then a second list of names is noted, all hopeful ones, but they are to wait yet longer. Then comes the *solitary* case of discipline during their first years of church-life. This is painful, because it is the first, but one wherein only the temper has failed. To-night, after three months of separation, the breach is healed. Now comes a talk of the future. The missionary is failing; he feels his growing weakness. Johnson is shown how he must be the pastor,

---

* Joseph Fuller is a son of Alexander Fuller, one of the Jamaica immigrants, who died shortly after his arrival. This son is still living at Hickory or Mortonville, and serving the Lord with successful diligence and ardent zeal.

that he must begin the work now; buckle on the armour more firmly and stand, if the teacher falls.

"We change this scene again, and it is myself, wearied and faint and full of pain. This is not worth looking at. A poor faltering worm. But before I close to-night, let me ask, Will it be lawful for me to come home for a change at no distant day? I ask now because I know the time will soon come when I must take a change or die, and when the time comes I cannot wait for an answer. I hope to labour on a few months yet before I am broken down; and be assured of this, I cannot leave till stern duty drives me."

The needed relief was not only promptly granted by the Committee of the Society, but by the arrival of the Rev. Jno. Diboll, of Holt, Norfolk, towards the close of the year, as pastor of the church at Clarence, Mr. Saker was able in July, 1855, to obtain the change he so much required. Mrs. Saker, whose health had utterly broken down, as well as that of their little boy, had preceded him homewards in the February of the previous year. It was none too soon. For several days prior to his embarkation, he was so ill that his life was thought to be fast drawing to a close. It pleased God, during the voyage, to restore him in some measure to his usual health, so that on his arrival he was able to communicate to many friends in various parts of the country, in some detail, the progress and character of his work, and to deepen in the minds of the churches their interest in the salvation of Africa.

His stay in his native land was not a prolonged one. Ever anxious to be at the post of duty, Mr. and Mrs. Saker, after an interesting interview with the Committee, in which plans were arranged for the welfare of the Mission, sailed from Plymouth on the 24th of December (1855). The voyage, till their arrival at Madeira, was a tempestuous one; but on the 2nd of February (1856) they landed at Clarence, having enjoyed a passage which strengthened their health. A welcome was given scarcely inferior in the rapture of the greeting to that which met them on their return in 1850, when the converts had been bereaved of all their teachers. They found Mr. Diboll in good health, and with much to cheer him in his labour among the people of Fernando Po. At Cameroons the native brethren were persever-ingly carrying on the Lord's work. Writing on the 6th of February, Mr. Saker says, " This evening, at eight o'clock, we were permitted to arrive at our peaceful home, and to bow with Johnson and our young friends in thankful prayer, all of whom the Lord has mercifully preserved. Fuller is away at Bimbia, but I hear he is quite well."

Mr. Saker at once plunged into the full stream of active labour. With slight exception he found every-thing proceeding in a satisfactory manner. The state of the church was gratifying; Johnson's labours had been blessed. Seven persons had been admitted to the fellowship of the church, and there were many hopeful inquirers. As to Johnson, he says, " I need only say he is as he was, perhaps more humble; I cannot express my thankful feelings on finding him so well." " The name of N'kwe I note with much satisfaction. A letter written years since informed you of the baptism of several; one was specified as a prince, another as a slave. The former, under the honourable name of Thomas Horton, has been known in our books for some time; the other has trodden a very lowly path, but equally useful, till at last we have separated him for the work of an evan-

gelist. The whole country is at present his field of labour."
Mr. Saker was also happy to welcome a trained teacher
from Sierra Leone for the school, a young woman of
earnest piety and affectionate character, whom he had
sent thither some months before for education.

At Bell Town, in September, the house of the native
missionary was invaded by a rabble, incited by superstition. His wife was dragged out, her clothing torn off,
and she was taken with another woman into the bush.
Johnson, accompanied by some of his friends, pleaded
with the king till midnight for their liberation, and so
far succeeded as to have them placed in the house of his
nephew, who, with his wife, was a member of the church.
The next day superstitious rites were resumed, and pay-
ments were demanded to free the women from annoy-
ance. Ultimately, through Mr. Saker's intervention
and firmness, the women were released, and the aggres-
sors consented to pay a fine to recompense them for
their sufferings. "Thus we are permitted," says Mr.
Saker, after recounting the incident, "to enjoy a moral
triumph, a feeble and unprotected worm in the midst of
five thousand heathens contending and triumphing over
them. Why is this? Verily it is that the conscience
of the multitude is on our side. God constrains them
to bow to the work of a solitary teacher; and great is
the rejoicing in the town to-day that I have promised
to be their friend still. Yesterday was gloom and
sorrow; to-day, one of joy. Well it is for us when our
triumph is gladness for the multitude. This evening I
attend to receive the acknowledgment of the offending
chief."

It will already have become apparent with what deep
interest Mr. Saker studied the native tongue, and

laboured night and day to embody in a printed shape, for permanent use, the knowledge he had acquired. It was no slight task to acquire a barbarous language, having no written letter or character, without books to guide, or competent interpreters to translate. The patience, toil, and incessant correction needful for its successful prosecution few can estimate. It is only due, even at some length, to give in his own words a description of Mr. Saker's methods and their results. His letter is dated December 22nd, 1856 :—

"In my various translations and printing in the language which I have most to do with, I have made some considerable progress. The printing has conduced very much to give to my knowledge of the language such solidity as I think will now enable me to give it grammatical form and order. Through years of labour, not devoted wholly to this one thing, I have sought to lay hold of all the forms of speech as they fall from native lips, then to compare and separate those forms, and bring out classes of words and syllables.

"A mental structure at last arose from this chaos, and I wished to give the language that form in print it had assumed in my notes and books. I made a beginning, and printed eight pages; but a multitude of labours prevented my prosecuting it, until after many months my health failed so much as to compel me to prepare for visiting Europe. The uncertainty of life, and the consciousness that all my knowledge of the language would be lost to the mission, should I not survive my voyage, determined me to complete the grammar in as condensed a form as possible.

"In great weakness and oft in fever, the copy was written and the proofs corrected. The day before the mail was due, the last sheet was printed. The few lines of introduction were then written, and given to the printer at six in the evening; at midnight I arose and corrected the proof; at ten next morning a sufficient number of copies were stitched for me to carry to Europe. The mail did not come, and I had then to lie and suffer another month. How much weaker I became by that month's unmitigated fever, or how near to the grave when I at last left, it is not needful to think about. It is enough to know that the voyage home, the kind attentions of friends, and the innumerable mercies that God granted me through them, resulted in restoring me to health, and eventually to my labour in this land.

"Now that I am thus restored, and have been enabled to conquer some difficulties that have arisen in consequence of my absence, I am very desirous of completing the work which was then so imperfectly and so feebly attempted in weakness and pain.

"While in England I read through this small grammar, and although I saw many things imperfectly explained, and many not explained at all, I was satisfied with the general distinctness with which the leading facts of the language were exhibited. With the arrangement of the verb I was not satisfied, and could see that the whole needed revision. I remember but too distinctly the suffering in which it was put together, and I almost wished it had not been printed.

"A larger grammar I have now begun, and hope for health to finish it. It must have my undivided attention only occasionally, but I hope to complete it during the coming year.

"I have tried these first sixteen pages in some old type, and by picking the best of the letters it is readable; but I fear I shall be obliged to take my Scripture type, and use this old fount for school purposes as heretofore.

"You will remember the attention that was devoted to African philology in 1850, and the *rules* that were sent out, recommending missionaries to adopt one uniform orthography. As these *rules* made no change of consequence in my work, beyond the introduction of two new characters for previous diphthongs, I adopted them without difficulty. The attention given to this subject in the above year and since has, it seems, resulted in the publication of a *standard alphabet*. This alphabet I received about three months since, and have given it all the attention it needed; most of its statements will be generally approved.

"I have printed ten copies for correction, on writing paper, with a large margin; and if you will kindly make remarks on it, or propose any questionings to direct my attention to anything that may not be plain, I shall be grateful for the aid, and it may conduce much to the perspicuity of the grammar when done. This, of course, applies to the following sheets as much as this, for I intend to send you each sheet as it is prepared, if you can find time for its reading.

"I enclose four copies. If you think of any friends who are competent to offer an opinion, and at the same time can command leisure for the examination, I hope you will not hesitate to put one in their hands, and maybe their remarks will be of service."

The allusion here made by Mr. Saker to a "standard alphabet" refers to the result of a conference which met at the Prussian Embassy in the year 1850. It was summoned by the late Chevalier Bunsen, and consisted

of such eminent men as Professors Lepsius and Max
Müller, Professor Owen, and Sir Charles Trevelyan,
together with the Secretaries of the leading Missionary
Societies. Its object was to attain uniformity in the
use of Roman letters when, for the first time, any
African language is reduced to writing. By the
employment of this alphabet, which was based on
scientific and physiological principles, great progress
has been made in identifying and classifying the
languages of the African continent, and in the recognition of racial and linguistic affinities between the
innumerable tribes scattered over its vast surface. The
Dualla has been found to be only one dialect of a
tongue which, in its root forms, is known across the
entire continent, and from the banks of the Cameroons
to the borders of Zululand.* It is matter for regret
that this "standard alphabet" is not in every case
employed by those who are interested in Africa's
civilisation and evangelisation.

It is only necessary to add to the above striking
account of persistent and noble endeavour, that early in
the following year (1859) Mr. Saker had succeeded in
putting to press the Book of Psalms and the Epistle to
the Romans, and a few copies as specimens had been
struck off. He only awaited a supply of accents from
England to place these precious documents of God's
Word in the hands of the Dualla people.

---

* See on this interesting subject an important work just
published, entitled: "A Sketch of the Modern Languages of
Africa." By R. N. Cust, of H.M. Indian Civil Service. In 2
vols. London: Trübner. 1883.

CHAPTER IX.

THE HOME OF FREEDOM, 1858.

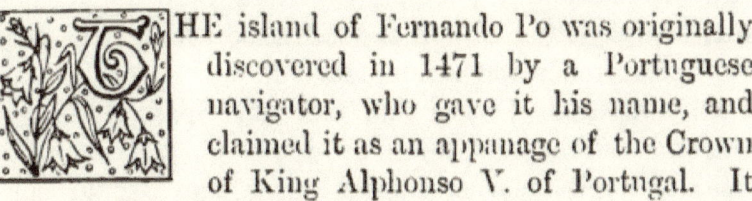THE island of Fernando Po was originally discovered in 1471 by a Portuguese navigator, who gave it his name, and claimed it as an appanage of the Crown of King Alphonso V. of Portugal. It was ceded to Spain in 1778, and, after a short occupation, it was abandoned by the Spanish Government in 1782. In 1827, the English Government formed a settlement on the north side of the island, naming it after the Duke of Clarence, who was then at the head of the Admiralty. The situation of the island furnished the English fleet with a convenient harbour from which to watch the coast, and to carry on the suppression of the slave traffic, in which beneficent work Great Britain was then actively engaged. The colonists consisted of two classes, those brought from Sierra Leone as artisans or labourers, for the most part employed in the service of the fleet, and others liberated from slave vessels by Her Majesty's cruisers; but all of them were British subjects and under English rule. Although, at the commencement of the Baptist Mission in 1841, it was known that the Spanish Crown had revived the claim to the sovereignty of the island, its representative, the Commander of the brig *Nervion*, Captain de Lerena, respected the British character of the colonists, and specially decreed,

on the part of Her Catholic Majesty's Government, that "personal liberty, property, and religion should be secure to every inhabitant." Under this liberal law the Mission was founded, and it was not until the year 1845 that any interference was attempted.

On Christmas Day of that year, the Spanish Consul-General arrived at Clarence. He was instructed to send the missionaries away, unless they would consent to reside "in a private capacity only." With this condition they declined to comply; but as the Consul regarded their labours as of great benefit to the people, he was willing to give them a year's grace in which to prepare for their departure. Meanwhile they might continue to preach, and to carry on their schools. Ultimately it was arranged that for an indefinite time there might always remain in Clarence one missionary and two teachers, but that the interior tribes should not be evangelised. With the Consul also came a bishop and a priest. Their efforts to attract the people by the "scenic display" of Roman Catholic rites utterly failed, and before the end of the year 1846 they returned to Spain. It is due to the bishop to say that he acknowledged in the warmest terms the benefits resulting from the labours of the missionaries, and published in Spain a grateful recognition of the advantages he had personally enjoyed from the medical attendance and advice of Dr. Prince. "In spite of all my endeavours," he says, "to recompense in a slender degree the generosity and watchfulness of Dr. Prince, I never could succeed in making him receive the smallest remuneration for his valuable services."

Contrary to the expectation of the missionaries, they were left with little molestation till the month of

6

September, 1856, when another bishop with several priests landed, with the avowed object of extinguishing the Mission and expelling the missionaries from the island. As they were not, however, armed with sufficient authority to set aside the arrangements made in 1845, the bishop soon left, and shortly afterwards the priests also, with the intention of obtaining enlarged powers from the Spanish Government.

At length, in the evening of Saturday, May the 22nd, 1858, the Spanish steam vessel *Balboa* anchored in Clarence Cove, having on board Don Carlos Chacon, Commander of the Spanish squadron, and Governor-General of all the islands belonging to Spain on the coast. With six Jesuits, he had come to give effect to the orders of the Spanish Crown. He proclaimed the religion of the Roman Catholic Church to be the sole religion of Fernando Po, as it was that of the kingdom of Spain, to the exclusion of every other. No other religious profession could be "tolerated or allowed." Professors of alien religions must confine their worship to their private houses, and limit it to the members of their families. The edict was read in a scanty audience of the people, with the firing of cannon, and amidst torrents of rain, the lightning and thunder of a tropical tornado giving a strange awfulness to the scene. That evening, the evening of the 27th of May, the people met for the last time in open worship to call upon God their Saviour.

That the measure was due in large degree to the restless activity and intrigues of the Society of Jesus there can be little doubt. But, besides this, the rapid growth of commerce in the Gulf of Guinea, and the opening of the great river Niger to European enterprise, had given increased value to the island of Fernando Po, holding as it does the key to the embouchure of the Niger and the command of the entire coast of the Gulf, with its tributary rivers, the Calabar and the Cameroons. The arrival of the Spaniards having thus put a stop to the public services of the sanctuary, on the Lord's-day afternoon, May 30th, Mr. Saker gathered a few of his flock in the wilderness behind Clarence, and, under the overhanging branches of the forest, conducted the worship of God. The weather was not propitious. Torrents of rain descended, and many were prevented from joining the assembly by the Romish priests, who paraded the streets of the town throughout the day. Many armed sailors also moved about, Governor Chacon having been informed by some adversary that the people were being urged to mutiny and insurrection. It was said that they would *fight* for their worship. Nevertheless, the day passed without disturbance; the voice of prayer and praise was heard in nearly every cottage, the proclamation forbidding public worship only in the chapel.

In repeated interviews, as well as by correspondence, Mr. Saker endeavoured to shake the resolution of the Commander. His reply to the request for permission to remain, reports Mr. Saker, was, in plain English, " I cannot; I will not grant it. Do not ask me again." The final answer of the Governor was read to the inhabitants in a public meeting called to receive it. Fearing interruption, there was not any open act of worship performed. At Mr. Saker's request, the assembly sat for a few minutes in silent prayer, and then, with deep solemnity of feeling, the resolve was taken to leave the island as soon as provision could be

G*

made for a new settlement, in a land where freedom
of conscience and civil liberty could be enjoyed.

As the entire abandonment of the Mission in Clarence
was imperative, a new home had now to be sought for
all who valued liberty and truth. No better pioneer in
the search could have been found than Alfred Saker,
and he was not slow to comprehend and to meet the
necessities of the case. After narrating the events that
had transpired, Mr. Saker writes to the Committee :—
" Now, as to the future, Jesus shall be our guide. There
are a few general ideas which I can put on paper. Pray
for us that we may be directed aright. Cameroons is
ours—a fine station, an open door to the interior of the
land. Bimbia is ours—room enough for a town, and
large trade. But a port is wanted, where there can be
British protection, British capital and laws ; a depot
for coals for the navy, a safe harbour for our merchant
vessels, a free port for the commerce of these rivers,
and a refuge for the oppressed and the slave. These
are all essential points to be secured, and I think are
all attainable, if the British Government can be so far
interested as to put their hands to the work. Then
there are matters specially missionary ; these will have
our careful attention. There is now no idea of remaining here. The long-endured oppression, the expected
threats of banishment, and the general decay of all
business, had determined many to leave before this.
Now our course must be, first, to provide a home for all,
if possible, where freedom to worship God must be the
first requirement ; and then, next, for employment, and,
if possible, prosperity."

His resolve was taken. Two days after penning this
letter, Mr. Saker set forth to explore the mountain region

of the Cameroons, which, with its rocky shores, bays, and islands, lay opposite, some twenty miles distant from Fernando Po.

Wednesday morning, the 2nd of June, was wet and gloomy; but, in company with Mr. Fuller, a native brother, five boys and two women, at eight o'clock Mr. Saker sailed in a small native craft for Bimbia. Heavy rain, chopping winds, with intervals of dead calm, delayed the vessel's progress. Worst of all, in the confusion occasioned by taking on board a large number of packages, the basket of provisions was left behind. The little tea and sugar they found had got mixed with pepper. Hungry, wet, and sick, the voyagers at length reached Bimbia on the following Sabbath. Four days and a-half had been spent in a voyage usually of twelve hours' duration.

King William, the Bimbia chief, had now to be seen, and his consent gained to the occupation of such a part of the coast as might be found suitable for a settlement. Previous journeys and voyages pointed out the Bay of Amboises as a favourable spot; and, at Mr. Saker's formal request, the chief willingly agreed to sell such a tract of land as might be wanted. He also promised a guide when the missionary was ready to start on his exploring expedition. The weather being very stormy, Mr. Saker proceeded to his station at Cameroons, where arrangements were requisite for the reception of some of the children from Clarence. The boat being provisioned, Mr. Saker left, on Monday, the 14th of June, for Bimbia. By nightfall the bar of the river was reached, where he anchored till next morning. A night of storms and of rolling seas, with great discomfort, followed. A small canoe that Mr. Saker had taken with

him was lost; but Bimbia was at length reached in the
afternoon.   After a hurried dinner, Mr. Saker, with Mr.
Fuller and a guide, set out to explore the bay, where he
hoped to find a suitable refuge for his flock. With rapid
steps they penetrated the wilderness, and soon, at War
Bay, came upon the sea, under the towering cliffs which
skirt its shores. The track round the bay was exceedingly difficult; they had to traverse broken rocks and
boulders innumerable, loose, rolling, with slippery surface
and jagged edge, the débris of mighty volcanic action.
Turning again into the wilderness, the path led them
across ravines and through rivers, over cliffs, and along
the base of the mountains, which here approach the sea.
The thick bush of the forest was dark as night; but the
level and open land exhibited a rich soil, well timbered
and watered.

The Bay of Amboises reached, it was too late to
explore it. The sun was setting, so the return journey
was begun. The dark wilderness was darker by night.
The guide lost his way. Then came the necessity of
forcing a path through the thick underwood. The rocks
had to be scrambled over by the light of the stars,
precipices avoided, and deep ravines crossed. Amid
these arduous exertions the night wore away. For six or
seven hours the weary wandering lasted. At length
the roar of the sea was heard. Trembling and thankful,
the perplexed travellers reached War Bay, but their
labours were far from done. "To walk over these
stones by the faint light of the stars," says Mr.
Saker, "was impossible, yet go we must. Weary
and sore we began. On my knees, my toes, and
with my hands, I laboured for two hours over
that dreadful road." The cliff reached, it was too dark

to find the path to ascend it; so, being safe from the tide, the travellers lay down, under God's protection, on the stones, and tried to sleep. " The cold was too great; Fuller and I lay close, to be warm; but we could not sleep. In about an hour and a half the first faint streak of morning aroused us. Soon, very soon, we found the track, and then we ascended. By half-past six we had reached Fuller's house at Bimbia." Shoes, trowsers, hat, umbrellas: all were torn or battered to pieces; their hands were pierced with thorns, and gashed by the sharp edges of the rocks.

The morning light also showed them that a few feet beyond the spot where they lay down there was a steep precipice. Surely the hand of God preserved them from taking in the darkness the few steps by which their lives would have been sacrificed.

Such was the first attempt to find in the wilderness a lodge for the people of God. But, undismayed by this perilous adventure, the indefatigable explorers took boat after breakfast, and set out for Amboises Bay by sea. In the Niger expedition of 1841, this bay was visited by Captain W. Allen, its commander. On several occasions his ships had anchored within the islands which shelter the entrance from the mighty swell of the great Atlantic; but the officers of the survey received the impression that, while the anchorage was safe, the climate salubrious, and the proximity of the mountains favourable to health, the bay did not contain a safe landing-place. Naught but a heavy surf was visible from the steamer's deck. " But now," says Mr. Saker, " that I need a home for our people, where a trade may be created, and to which commerce may be drawn, I search for a landing only; and, behold! God hath hidden, up a deep interior

bay, for ages—a bay with nearly two miles of beach—
without a stone, and almost without a wave, large enough
to contain a thousand boats and small vessels; while
the Amboises Bay will contain a navy. Into this bay
the sea-breeze blows in all its purity, and the mountain
wind at night is all freshness. Here, if Her Majesty's
Government sanction and sustain our efforts, can be put
up coal stores, provision stores, building-yards, and every
other essential for commerce. Here, too, a highway may be
made into the interior, and the native produce be shipped
in smooth water for Europe. It will be a centre of
civilisation, freedom, and light. It will be essentially a
religious, enlightened colony. And here, also, under
British protection, the Lord's people may worship God
without molestation."

During a lovely day the exploration of this beautiful
retreat was completed. The toil of the previous days
was forgotten in the success which had been achieved;
and the missionary returned to Clarence with a glad and
grateful heart to report to his brethren how the good
hand of God had led him and prospered his way. On
his arrival in Clarence, Mr. Saker found in the little
harbour three more Spanish men-of-war.

Ambas, or Amboises Bay, is situated to the north-
east of Fernando Po, and is shadowed by the volcanic
mountains of the Cameroons, the highest peak of which
rises, within ten or twelve miles of the sea, to the height
of 13,760 feet. Three islands occupy its entrance; Abobbi
or Pirate Island, Dameh or Ambas Island, and Men-
doleh. Of these, the last is the largest, and is covered
with forest trees to its highest point. All are inhabited by
a race evidently derived from Bimbia, and they speak a
modification of the Dualla language. They claim to be

independent of the chiefs of the continent, and their independence is secured by the rocky fastnesses in which they dwell.

Somewhat numerous tribes, known as the Bakwili people, dwell among the mountains, and bring the produce of their cultivation for exchange with the Isubu and other tribes dwelling in the lowlands of the Bimbia country, and with the islanders of the Bay.

Once within the shelter of the islands, the voyager sees before him a bay some fifteen to twenty miles in circuit, with a rocky shore, and the surf perpetually breaking upon it. An opening in the rocky ridge to the eastward admits boats and small vessels into a cove, revealing an open space, with a fine sandy beach, nearly two miles in length, by a mile and a half in breadth, watered by a deep and copious mountain stream. Mr. Saker fixed on this spot for the new settlement and mission station, which he named Victoria. The outer bay has a safe anchorage for ships of a large size at all seasons, and is open only to the south-west wind, blowing cool and refreshing from the broad Atlantic. The first eminence on the way to the great Cameroons mountain rises within three or four miles of the cove, and reaches to the height of 5,820 feet. Its sides are clothed with forest. Old men relate that fire was seen years ago to issue from the main peak. They felt the earth "shake like a steamboat." This, coupled with the local name of the mountain, Mongo-ma-lobah, or God's mountain, lends probability to the supposition that it may be the chariot of the gods spoken of by Hanno the Carthaginian.*

---

* Capt. W. Allen's "Niger Expedition," vol. i., p. 273.

Here Mr. Saker resolved to found a colony of African Pilgrim Fathers, where the true worship of God might freely and uninterruptedly be observed, the rights of conscience be secured from the intrusion of Romish intolerance, and a new pharos of spiritual light be erected for the illumination of the surrounding tribes.

Mr. Saker and his companions soon tested the salubrity of the spot, and the excellence of the water, which, in an abundant stream, flows into the sea at the western end of the cove. " I went there," he says, " with my company in my usual health, or rather ill-health, strong enough for work, but with little energy ; a ceaseless craving for food, yet no appetite; eating just enough to live. This is constant. In that state I went to Victoria, and I began to feel the effects of its air the first day. My appetite returned and increased. At night I slept with my whole heart, equally as with my whole heart I do my daily working. Rest was sweet, food was sweet ; life was life, and not a dying death."

The property in the soil having already been secured,* Mr. Saker at once commenced his preparations to colonise it. Returning to Cameroons, he quickly brought together the materials for a small hut, and, accompanied by a band of men and boys drawn from

---

* " District of land commencing at War Bay, and by coast line embracing the headland Mananga, Foo Bay, Ambas Bay, to the point of land called Kokki, including the islands Mondovi, N'Aami, and Bohu ; thence inland towards the Great Mountain five miles ; thence by line to the town of Bosambo ; thence to M'janji on the Bimbia River till parallel with the Albert Hills ; and thence embracing these hills the line shall enter a rivulet running to War Bay." The above description is copied from King William's grant. The original is in possession of the Society.

the stations on the river, he proceeded to erect it on the selected site. "On the 9th of June," he says, "we went on shore at Amboises Bay. Of this land we took possession with prayer. By seven in the evening we had a tenantable abode, nine feet by eighteen. There we then assembled for united worship; and there nineteen of our company laid down to sleep that night, while I, and three of my boys, retired to the boat."

In constant wind and rain, with short intermissions of fine weather, the labour of clearing the ground went on. The two first trees were felled by Mr. Saker's own hands. "In one day," he says, "there fell twenty-seven trees of the dense forest, and very much of the impenetrable underwood." Slowly the rude hut on the beach was enlarged, other buildings for stores were put up, and sections of them were divided into apartments for families as they might arrive from Clarence. "On Friday, the 13th," he says, "we began our public worship, with very fervent prayers that the worship might be continued, and be pure through coming generations, and that the Gospel there might be the light of life to thousands. Then, again, on the Sabbath we had our three services, as at Clarence in former days. A prayer meeting on Monday evening, and class on Wednesday and preaching on Friday. Thus the public worship of the tabernacle is begun, and I hope never to cease till the angel announces the ' *end of time.* ' "

As the work proceeded the situation was found to surpass their expectations. The harbour was well protected from seaward by lines of rock, and afforded abundant space for wharves, docks, and landing piers. The land was everywhere raised above the highest tides. The river gave an unfailing supply of the purest

water. With characteristic skill and energy Mr. Saker
satisfied himself of its abundance. "I measured it,"
he says, "and found 27,000 cubic feet of water flowing into the ocean every minute. Its clear stream shows
two things—first, that its course is over a rocky bed;
second, that land floods, which would be muddy, do
not swell the volume into a turbid bounding torrent.
The land floods evidently find an outlet in another
river I visited." The first road laid out ran from
Morton Bay to this ever-flowing stream. It consti-
tuted the first street, and was 5,480ft. long. In the
centre of it a plot was measured off for the chapel, and
building lots, each one hundred feet in depth by fifty in
breadth, were staked out on either side. A fence was
planted to protect the township from the dense forest
behind, and from the wild animals which have their
home beneath its gigantic trees. Names were given to
the various points around. Morton Bay was named
after Sir Morton Peto. A mount, 800ft. high, about a
mile from the landing-place, with a rocky face towards
the Bay, was named Helena, after his absent but beloved
wife. Another elevation, east of the town, 2,000ft.
high, clothed with richest foliage to the summit, acquired
the name of Mount Henry, after his excellent friend,
the late Henry Kelsall, Esq.

In addition to the general salubrity of the spot, it was
found that the natives of the mountain came every
third day to a market that was held on the level
beach. It was a provision market. Here the plantains,
palm nuts, and yams of the interior were exchanged for
salt, tobacco, and for the fish caught and cured and
dried by the inhabitants of the islands. The new settlers
were spared those privations which Mr. Saker and his

BIRD'S-EYE VIEW OF VICTORIA, AMBOISES BAY, WEST AFRICA.

family endured on their first arrival in the Cameroons river. "There is," he remarks, "abundance on the mountain, and the fish at our command will cause the mountain produce to come down to us. And as to price, a small fish is demanded for a yam or a bunch of plaintains, for which at Cameroons I must pay a shilling." The great advantages the settlement possessed may be summed up in Mr. Saker's own words: " The vast importance to us of a sanatorium I need not speak of to you; I entertain hopes the most sanguine. This comes unexpectedly to me. I have mentally seen it—Victoria—a centre of freedom, of light, of education, and commerce. It is also a highway into the interior. This has been its highest glory in my eyes. If in addition to this it shall be a refreshing, reviving locality, how great will be the advantage! how large our mercy!"

The township planned by Mr. Saker for the exiles from Clarence lay wholly on the eastern side of the stream; the western side he reserved with the hope that here might be built the store-houses and wharves which would be required should the British Government make Amboises Bay the centre of their operations on the coast.

The arrival of the settlers from Clarence rendered necessary some regulations by which the infant colony should be governed, and which might afford a firm foundation for its growth and prosperity. Perhaps in nothing was the sagacity and wisdom of Mr. Saker more prominent than in the laws which he laid down for their guidance and control. The document that he prepared will be found in the Appendix, but some of its chief features must be noticed here. After stating that the township of Victoria had been purchased from the King of Bimbia, and the right and title thereto ceded to its present possessors, he declares that the township had been formed "as a refuge and a home for those who cannot continue where liberty of worship is denied, and for all others who may be desirous of living peacefully with us." Following this statement are directions as to the purchase and possession of the plots marked out in the town, and then "laws" are enacted for the government of the colony. The government is to be carried on by a Governor and Council, who will have power over all roads and thoroughfares, and enforce, under certain penalties, the regulations that may be agreed upon. The following important constitutional principle is affirmed :— "There shall be entire freedom in all that relates to the worship of the true God, and the Word of God is hereby acknowledged to be the foundation of all our laws, and claims the obedience of our lives. Although we are now all of one mind in the essentials of Christian worship, yet should there come among us persons of differing opinions as to Christian worship and duty, all shall equally share in the freedom of worship, as well as in our protection." The Sabbath is declared to be a day of rest, and all business must be suspended to allow of its enjoyment, and the uninterrupted worship of God. Freedom of trade is secured, and a free importation permitted of all articles of commerce, excepting spirits of every kind. These articles can only be permitted to enter for medicinal purposes, or, if for any other object, under a duty of ten per cent. But their sale or barter is not permitted at all. Other regulations follow, one especially reserving power to institute and ordain laws as occasion may require.

Under these wise, simple, but efficient rules, the

colony has grown to its present condition of prosperity.
Not that it has realised yet all that its founder anticipated. To use his own trustful words, "For it I toiled
day and night; I have worn my spirits down to a wafer's
weight; my eyes and hands too." This was literally
true. With his own hands he showed the exiles how to
build their houses. He planned the structures that
slowly rose from the midst of the bush, which he was
amongst the first to clear away. He was resolved that
on that spot God should be freely worshipped, and the
servants of the Lord have a secure home. As the result,
some hundreds of Africa's children now enjoy perfect
freedom of body and mind. The voice of praise and
prayer rises unceasingly on the mountain air, and the
schools are ever training their children to enjoy the
blessings that a Christian civilisation can impart. Slowly
the tribes of the hills around are coming under Christian
influence, and important steps have been taken to reach
the far interior. Commerce is gradually spreading its
beneficent interchanges among the people under the
protection of the British flag, which, from time to time,
floats in the convenient bay. If the promise of Colonel
Nichols has not yet been fulfilled, it is nevertheless
probable that at no distant date the Imperial Crown of
England will exercise the sovereignty which the inhabitants of Victoria would gladly recognise and obey.*

---

* Years ago the Bimbia chief, William, surrendered the sovereignty of his country to Colonel Nichols, as the representative
of the British Crown, and received from him the empty title of
King, in which his son still rejoices. The act of Col. Nichols has,
however, never been formally acknowledged by the Government
of Great Britain, although its cruisers and men-of-war frequently
visit the coast, and arbitrate among the tribes in cases of difficulty
and war.

Looking back at the close of this eventful year, Mr Saker could gratefully say: "A year of change and of toil. Storms have beat on us, yet He has preserved us. Nor sun nor moon has been permitted to smite. In doubt or perplexity, if it has once crossed our pathway, He speedily removed it, and, in the labours of each succeeding hour, He has more than supported and sustained our powers. God has opened for us a wide door at Victoria, Amboises Bay. This is now our refuge, and already the wilderness begins to rejoice. Its swelling hills and noble mountain range tell of freedom, fertility, and health. No Jesuitical craft nor Spanish intolerance will darken its increasing brightness. There, through the mercy of our redeeming Lord, we shall worship and adore till this mortal sinks and the immortal spirit soars beyond the mountain to the Throne of God."

In view of the work achieved by this devoted missionary of the Cross, the language of the Society's Report, in 1860, is not a whit too strong:—"It is difficult suitably to describe Mr. Saker in his varied labours; and when his early circumstances are considered, and his present extraordinary attainments, some of them reaching to the higher departments of science, he seems to be not only eminently fitted for his post, but to be one of the remarkable men of the age."

MISSION HOUSE AND SCHOOL, AMBOISES BAY, CAMEROONS.

CHAPTER X.

URING the sixteen months which followed the close of the year 1858, the necessities of the Mission required Mr. Saker to be constantly on the move from one station to another. The arrival of the Rev. J. Diboll at Victoria in April, 1859, enabled him, however, to relinquish the charge of the congregation and schools there, and personally to superintend the removal and settlement of a portion of the Clarence people in their new home. The return of Mrs. Saker and his daughter Eliza from England secured the progress of his work on the Cameroons, and the appointment of the Rev. J. Pinnock, of Jamaica, to a new station at Abo, higher up the river, gave hope of the extension of the Gospel to the inner parts of the country. The printing of the Scriptures was diligently carried on, and the indefatigable missionary had the pleasure of seeing through the press his translation of the Book of Psalms, and a small collection of hymns, in the Dualla language. He records that he "had so far impressed his ideas of work on others that all the sheets have been printed while he was visiting or preaching at other places." The binding also was the work of native lads, who only a few years before had been rescued from barbarism. Respecting the composition of the hymns, and also of

7

many of the tunes sung to them, Mr. Saker gives the following interesting account in a letter to the Rev. F. Trestrail, February 29th, 1860:—"I am no poet. In early life, like some others, I wrote doggerel; but, for the Africans, we are obliged to do our best in everything, and then fear no censor. I have written what is *literally* thus—

> "'O Son of God, to Thee,
> To Thee Thyself we come;
> With prayer we bend to Thee,
> With praises, too, we bend.'

> "3rd ver. 'Through Thee, Thyself alone,
> We live; in peace we live.
> Through Thee, Thyself alone,
> We tread our weary way.'

"As to the greater number of the hymns, they are rude renderings of our own hymns. But, in the attempt, my own feelings have dictated something more free, so that the translations are not really such, but may rather be called imitations.

"I will try to get Eliza to send you one or more of *my tunes.* Do not let this surprise you, for I am a lover of music. And although I have never allowed my compositions to go out of the house, I get more careless as I get into years, and the praise or blame of men will be alike indifferent to me now. Some of my best tunes are in daily use in our congregations in Africa; but it is not generally known that they are mine. On my way to Amboises Bay—my first visit—after a terrible day at sea, we reached Bimbia; and at night, while lying restless in my bed, I found myself singing one of our solemn but sweet hymns, but to a strange tune in my own fashion, and the thought came, perhaps it was the whisper of sleepless spirits: 'Yes, thou art a sweet melody for such solemn words'—so I rose up and put it on paper. The next day being Sabbath day, I sang it with that same hymn in our morning worship. The natives are fond of singing, and they follow readily in everything like natural music. A few days later I called this tune 'Victoria,' because it was the first time we sang it at the new home. The same day, and the same midnight hour, gave birth to another more solemn. It is called 'Helena.' Both were sung at Bimbia at the same service."

The decease of Mrs. Diboll on the 16th March (1860), combined with his entire loss of strength, constrained the bereaved husband to take a voyage to Teneriffe, and subsequently to his native land. In reference to these events Mr. Saker wrote : " I am again alone with God. He will not fail me." Not a European helper was left in the field to share with him the toils and the anxieties of the work. His own health also was in a shattered, if not perilous, state, and the thought often passed through his mind, should he be taken away, how could he best provide for the great interests in his charge ? Other circumstances, moreover, urged him to make a brief visit to England, in order to confer with the Committee, and by personal explanations assist in the decision to which it was necessary that the Committee should come. The Spanish Government still delayed the settlement of the claims of the Society for compensation for the property confiscated at Fernando Po. Her Majesty's Plenipotentiary to the Court of Spain was then most opportunely in England, and the case could fully, in all its aspects, be brought before him. At the same time, Mr. Saker would be able

7*

to remove certain unfavourable impressions that had been
made on the minds of some valued friends in England,
with regard to the methods he had pursued in carrying
forward the evangelisation and civilisation of the savage
tribes among whom his lot was cast.   On the 30th of
April he therefore took his passage in the mail for
England, and much refreshed by this voyage, he landed
at Liverpool on the 19th of June, with the Rev. J.
Diboll, whom he had overtaken at Teneriffe.

Without delay the two brethren laid before the Committee, in the fullest detail, every department of the
Mission, and the transactions incident to the formation
of the settlement in Amboises Bay.   In the resolutions
which were adopted on the 18th of July, the past and
future were referred to.   It was resolved—1. "That this
Committee desire to express to the Rev. A. Saker, and
the brethren associated with him in the African Mission,
and who have so effectually assisted him, their gratitude
for his strenuous and able efforts to meet the difficulties
arising out of the Spanish seizure of the Society's
property at Fernando Po."*   2. "That this Committee
deem it of the highest importance to secure one or more
additional missionaries for the African Mission, and that
it be referred to the African Sub-Committee to take
immediate steps to effect that object."

---

* It was not till the 23rd April, 1861, that Sir Morton Peto was
informed by the Foreign Office that the Spanish Government had
consented to pay £1,500 as a final settlement of the Society's
claims, "on account of the expulsion of the missionaries from
Fernando Po in 1858." A few months afterwards the money
reached the hands of the Treasurer. The cost, however, of the
removal of the buildings, and the purchase of the land on
Amboises Bay, exceeded £2,000.

Thus, in full view of the losses the Mission had sustained, the perils necessarily incident to the work, the costliness of the endeavours to introduce the Gospel and its attendant blessings among uncultured and savage people, Mr. Saker's heart was cheered by the confidence placed in him by the Committee, and by the resolve to continue the conflict with superstition and sin among the fierce and degraded tribes of Africa. The clouds lifted, and a bright hope sprang up in his mind of successful enterprise and Divine success.

By the end of October, the health of Mr. Saker and Mr. Diboll was so much improved as to justify their return. They were joined by the Rev. Robert Smith, a member of the congregation in Regent Street, Lambeth, and by Captain Milbourne, who took charge of the schooner the Committee had purchased to convey the missionaries, and to aid them in their work on the waters of the Cameroons and Amboises Bay.

On the 31st of October, the *Wanderer* left her moorings in the Bay of Dublin, and, after eleven days of various weather, the voyagers safely reached the island of Madeira. The entire passage to their destination occupied fifty-two days. In the evening of the 19th of December, the party, vigorous and hopeful, landed at Cameroons. "The voyage," says Mr. Saker, "has not been a long one, nor has it been unpleasant. We were able to continue our worship twice and thrice a day with very few exceptions. Our health, too, was uninterrupted, and in health and in peace, in strong hope, we land at this our home." He found Mrs. Saker and his family also well, and, after five busy days at Bethel, he started for Victoria. In a few brief, vigorous sentences, he sums up the result of his observations and inquiries.

"A brief investigation of all these places has given me mingled feelings of grief and gladness. Sin reigns where we hoped for righteousness. Oh, may the power of sin be broken soon! Faithful labour has been rewarded and accepted, and in this we rejoice. The schools, where established, are succeeding. Our brethren, Fuller, Pinnock, Johnson, and N'Kwe have laboured with much diligence and zeal; and our teachers, During, Decker, and my daughter, have succeeded well."

The little band of workers had had a trying time during his absence. Mr. Pinnock had been driven from Abo by the violence of the people, and all his possessions seized and distributed among them. War had broken out among the tribes on the river, and the mission family at Bethel had been horrified by the slaughter of a native, and the parading of his head and arms, dripping with blood, through the settlement. Women and girls had been kidnapped by traders in the river, and the renewal of the horrid abominations of the slave trade were only checked by the timely arrival of Her Majesty's Consul with a man-of-war. "One day," writes Mrs. Saker, "our native teacher N'Kwe brought home a poor creature from the town where he preaches on the Sabbath, to whom the people had given the poison drink. A chief's child had died, and, as two or three of her own children had also died, she was accused of witchcraft. These things do not occur so frequently as a few years ago, but they are very sad. I gave her medicine, and she recovered. This is the third we have been enabled to save from death since I came from England last year." A little later Mrs. Saker continues: "A day or two after, the mothers from the town were running to me begging me to take their little girls, and to rescue their chief, who was in irons. The people had sent slaves for his redemption, but the trader refused to take any but girls. I cannot tell you, dear sir, the grief of my heart to see the poor creatures, and to remember that a white man, an Englishman, was causing all this sorrow. I rescued three children. Two are still with me; one I was obliged to give up to the woman who brought her, for men surrounded the house in search for her. Mr. Fuller told them they must remove him by force before any one else should be taken from the Mission ground." The missionaries, true to their vocation, were the protectors of the poor, the defence of the oppressed, and the refuge of those that had no helper.

The reinforcements that Mr. Saker had brought with him, and the further addition of the Rev. J. Peacock later on in the year, enabled him to arrange both for the conduct of the stations already formed, and for the preaching of the Word in several neighbouring towns. But to Mr. Saker these accessions of strength brought no diminution of toil, but rather an increase of it, from the superintendence everywhere necessary. Mr. Peacock, shortly after his arrival, in a few graphic sentences, permits us to see this heroic man at work: "Amidst bodily infirmities and pain he does not stop. He moves like machinery, day by day, in the great cause of our gracious Master. I will just give an outline of his movements. In the day, early, you will find him translating. You may look for him: he is at the forge, like a blacksmith. Then you may see him at the cases in the printing-office, composing. Then it may be he is drawing plans of some work he wishes to be done; then searching the Hebrew to translate some important

text ; then preaching in Dualla to the natives. Indeed,
I could not tell the varied duties he performs daily.
How can I but esteem—yea, love—such a one, whose
heart is so engaged in the work to promote the glory of
God in this place. Truly he was raised up for a great
work, and, amidst all the difficulties that surround him,
he accomplishes his work as a workman that needeth
not to be ashamed."

It is obvious that missionary life, under such circumstances as have been detailed, cannot be carried on as in
more favoured climes. "I do not wish," says Mr. Peacock again, "to undervalue pulpit duties and good
preaching ; but a man that could do no more would be
a sorry workman on the West Coast of Africa." The
ripe fruits of civilisation cannot be gathered without
arduous and continuous toil. In these regions all trade
is barter, and it is only by gifts of beads, cloth, tobacco,
and the like that the missionaries can obtain the fruits
of the earth for food. If they want a house, they must
build it. They must be both workmen and the instruc-
tors of workmen. In other lands the missionary, if he
only has money, can have all his wants supplied. In
Africa he must be his own purveyor, his own carpenter
and brickmaker, and money is of no use. Inevitably
his day is occupied with manifold so-called secular pursuits, as well as with exertions for the attainment of his
great object—the evangelisation of the people. In these
regions the Gospel must go hand in hand with the arts
of civilised life, and the missionary must become the
pioneer of both.

In the month of June (1862) Mr. Saker was able to
report the completion at press of his version of the New
Testament into the Dualla tongue. "You will rejoice

with me," he says, writing to the Secretary on the 30th, " that God has enabled me to bring the last sheet of the New Testament through the press. The deluging rains, which confine one so much at home, have contributed to this result sooner than I expected; but other work which I hoped to complete before the 1st of August has been impeded to the same extent. I shall entrust a copy of the Epistles, with the Revelation, to the captain of the mail vessel, if he will deliver it in Liverpool without charge. You will rejoice, too, that my health is so much better. During the last month, I have been permitted to work at least five days in the week, and am now better than at the beginning. At the end of the Revelation I have appended ' weights, measures, and coins,' and remarks. I enclose a first-proof from the printer's case as far as composed. The additions to be made to-morrow go to show that the ancient cubit was only 18 inches. To this will be added the Dualla measures, which in this respect do not differ much from the Hebrew."

In a letter to Sir Morton Peto, dated a month later, Mr. Saker gives some additional information relative to the use of the translation :—" About the middle of June, cur merciful Lord enabled me to complete the translation and printing of the New Testament. Since then I have had about 200 copies bound, and these are now in the hands of our rising reading population. To bring these pages to the ears of the people, we have appointed an hour, four evenings in the week, for reading, with such explanations as may be needed. On the Sabbath, in the intervals of worship, we have two other meetings in the town, with crowded houses, simply for reading and prayer. My daughter conducts one, and our Mr. Smith the other. It will be gratifying to you to learn that Mr. Smith is all that I could hope of him. He assists me nobly and well. Some recent visits he paid to the interior towns fill him with hope of success, while painful experience is gradually teaching him that that success must only be looked for as the result of soul-trying labour."

Reference is here made to some terrible scenes of cruelty and degradation of which Mr. Smith was witness, and in which he was compelled to interfere, not without peril of his life. On reaching a town a mile up the river, the firing of guns was heard. The people of the town were shooting the wives and slaves of the subject people working on their farms. A fight ensued with the husbands of the assaulted women. Mr. Smith, under a burning sun, amidst the dropping shots of the musketry, hastened, at the desire of the chief, with a messenger to stay the shedding of blood. Two men only were killed, but many were wounded. After some days, with efficient help from Mr. Saker, peace was restored. A little later two innocent men were seized and brought to the landing place near the Mission house, to be drowned or murdered, and, as Mr. Smith was endeavouring to arrest the cruel purpose of their captors, he received a blow from behind, which made him stagger to the ground; but several of the native converts caught and supported him. Happily his hurt proved but of temporary inconvenience. Other like incidents sorely tried the courage of the young missionary, but the true spirit of self-sacrifice animated him. "My love for the work and the people increases the more I come in contact with them; and they, on the other hand, know how to love and trust those that sympathise with them in their various troubles. Notwithstanding their deep degradation, and dark heathen practices, they appear keenly to feel a wrong, and to appreciate an act of kindness, and this opens the way for making known to them the everlasting Gospel."

The completion of the New Testament, and in a few months that of a vocabulary, affords a favourable opportunity to give the results of Mr. Saker's investigations into the origin of the Dualla language and people.

The language is spoken by a population variously estimated as consisting of 30,000 to 80,000 persons, living about the mouth of the Cameroons river and the base of the great mountain which dominates the entire region. The people are thought to be a small part of a large family that at an early period migrated southward from Abyssinia, and spread themselves over five or six degrees of country to the north and south of the equator. Their original language has been broken up into many dialects, and with many of their tribes the traces of their origin have entirely disappeared. Among rude and unlettered people language undergoes rapid mutations, and attains forms that baffle all investigation. Still there exists evidence that the Dualla has many and close affinities with the languages of Eastern Africa, and with that of the tribes on the Gaboon.

Dualla is the name both of the people and of the tongue they speak. Their traditions are but few, and of no remote date. They refer their origin to one of the two sons of a man who settled on the western side of the Cameroons mountain. One, named Koli, remained in the parental seat; but the other, Dualla, crossed the region now known as Victoria and Bimbia, and expelled the Basas from their dwellings on the Cameroons river.

Marks of the contest are still seen in some embankments near the Mission station at Bethel. The river is said to have been narrower than at present, having within the last forty years made great encroachments on the land.

The Duallas are divided into tribes, under independent chiefs. Feuds are frequent, and property is very insecure. The slave trade was once the calling of the entire people, and to the rapine, oppression, and bloodshed of that fearful time, together with the diminution in the number of people consequent upon it, may be traced the ferocity so frequently witnessed by Mr. Saker and his companions. Since the cessation of the foreign slave trade, there has been a great improvement, and many wasted spots are recovering the population they had lost. Slaves are, however, still held among the people. They are usually the fruit of war, sometimes of purchase, and the labour of the field is usually carried on by them, as well as by the wives of the free portion of the population. In most Dualla towns the slaves are two to one in excess of the freemen. They are, in fact, from their number, which is continually increasing by births, treated rather as serfs than slaves, and the chiefs are in constant dread of an uprising among them.

The Dualla tongue has many affinities with the Isubu, spoken at Bimbia. Northward, and on the sides of the mountain, the languages differ from the Dualla, and the population has a different origin; but nearness and intercourse are fast breaking down the distinction. The Dualla vocabulary is very scanty as compared with more cultivated tongues. It contains about 2,400 root forms. It is, however, notwithstanding the

efforts of the missionaries, very imperfectly known.
"Ever and anon," says Mr. Saker, "we come upon
words which lie like grains of gold in the bed of the
stream, and, like grains, are revealed only by the disturbance of storms and floods. While the daily con-
cerns of man run smoothly on, in a few words he
expresses his wants, his thoughts and emotions; but
let his heart be moved by strong passion, by deep distress, by mental conflicts, and words none suspected to
be in his memory, or even in existence, are found
welling up from the deeps of his heart, and in a moment
we see that they are the true words—such words that a
less exciting cause would not have revealed." Often,
too, on some distant journey, and among some offshoot
of the same stem, he has picked up words for his vocabulary which were unused or unknown among the
tribes immediately around him.

The elementary sounds in Dualla are thirty-three in
number, which English letters, with some orthographical
additions, have been employed to express; excepting
c, h, q, and z, the sounds of which letters are unknown.

To this may be added the interesting fact, that all the
books hitherto printed in the Dualla tongue, with the
exception of the last edition (1882) of the New Testament, have all been printed on the spot, and chiefly by
lads trained in the Mission, the fruit of missionary
labour. The new edition of the New Testament just
referred to has been carried through the press
by Miss Emily Saker, Mr. Saker's youngest and highly
estimable daughter, now labouring with the devotion
and perseverance of her father at the station, and among
the people, so dear to his heart.

CHAPTER XI.

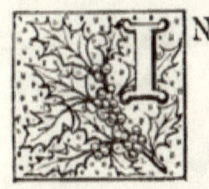N the last days of the year and the first weeks of 1862, Mr. Saker enjoyed a pleasant interlude in his work by the ascent of the great Cameroons mountain, having for his companions Captain Burton, H.M.'s Consul, M. Gustave Mann, a well-known Hanoverian and botanist, in the employment of the English Government, and Señor Calvo, the Spanish Judge of Fernando Po. Mr. Mann left Victoria on the 13th of December (1861) for the last town on the mountain, and on the arrival of the Consul with Señor Calvo on the 19th, Mr. Saker commenced the ascent with them, taking Mr. Johnson as interpreter, and several Kroomen to carry the luggage. The distance of the summit from Amboises Bay, on its southern side, is reckoned at 14 miles, but the mountain in its entire extent covers an area of about 400 square miles, between the Bimbia and Rumby rivers, which bound it on the east and west, and the hilly region that embraces it on the north. This was not the first attempt to climb the peak. Mr. Merrick assailed it in 1847, and succeeded so far as to reach the open grassy plain above the forest that covers the lower slopes of the mountain. Here water failed him; his companions suffered from cold and thirst, and he was compelled to return. In 1860, Mr. Mann ascended

CAMEROONS MOUNTAIN, AS SEEN FROM THE BROOK, VICTORIA.

a short distance, but time would not then allow further progress, and the mountain " whose glorious pinnacle never yet felt the foot of man " remained for the present party to climb its steeps, and to secure the long-coveted honour of being the first to tread this virgin peak.

The route from Victoria lay through a noble forest of palms, acacias, African oak, and other fine timber-trees, from 100 to 150 feet high, across a country admirably adapted for the growth of maize, cocoa, sugar, and coffee. Twice the party forded the " bright little mountain stream which supplies Victoria with the purest water," passing west of Mount Henry, " a site," says Captain Burton, " which I at once fixed upon as a provisional sanatorium." After four hours' walking, they halted for breakfast at Bosumba, a village of the chief Myombi, 1,000 feet above the sea and four miles and a-half from Victoria.

The path now led through dense bush and grass. The district was populous. The people are known as the Bakwili, and are allied by language and race to the tribes of the lowlands. Mr. Saker found that they understood the Isubu when he addressed them in that tongue. As usual, their dress was the scantiest possible, a kilt of plantain leaves sufficing for every need. A few possessed slips or rags of stuff or cloth, and a handker-chief for the head. Their ornaments, more abundant than their dress, were of beads of many colours, porcu-pine's teeth, and armlets of copper or brass, and occa-sionally of ivory. The head was bare, shaved, or, when otherwise, the hair was dressed in fantastic modes. A kind of axe, called a matchet, was carried by the men, and in a few cases a rusty old matchlock was the weapon of protection or offence. The women, as among all these tribes, performed not only every household duty, but carried on the cultivation of the ground, and were often tattooed in a fashion the most grotesque.

At half-past four they reached Maponya, in the country of the chief Botani, and the highest village in this part of the mountain. Here they met Mr. Mann. The chief received them with great ceremony. Habited in his royal garb, a tall black hat, an old scarlet and gamboge coatee of the Royal Marines, and a pocket handkerchief, " he performed a lively dance, apparently borrowed from the movements of excited poultry. In Africa, when the king dances, you have to pay for the honour."

Disputes arising with the natives, the party soon launched themselves on the wilderness. They bivouacked in the forest, on a steep and narrow spot, at a place afterwards called Ridge Camp. Proceeding at eight o'clock next day, they found that the plantain and the palm had disappeared, and were replaced by the graceful tree-fern. Ferns everywhere in most graceful forms covered the ground, or ran, creeper-like, up the trunks of the trees. It was "a beautiful fernery, set off by the huge tropical growth around it."

Passing under a natural arch of fallen trees, which they called Fern Gate, they emerged on a region of tall grass. Then came a broad green slope of small ferns and moss, resting on a rugged bed of old, decayed lava, half-a-mile wide, the banks on either side girt with giant trees. Here they breakfasted, and feasted on blackberries. A hunter's path now led them up the side of the lava river, among huge blocks which endangered their ancles. Salvias scented the air, and the surface was spangled with the blossoms of an unknown flower. Bees settled upon them, but did not sting; and the heat of the sun became intense.

The last part of the day's journey was the most rugged of all. The lava, as it approached the place of its issue, became more broken, lying about in most irregular heaps. Before attempting it, Captain Burton lay down to sleep, the rest of the party going on. The Black Crater, from which the lava had flowed, was at length reached. It was about 100 yards in diameter, with a lip of some 200 feet above the level of the platform below. On placing his compass between the rocks, Mr. Saker found that, in an unaccountable manner, the north pole of the needle dipped to the south. Water was obtained near at hand, and here the travellers encamped. It was a bad camping-place; a high north-east wind roared round them all night, and the thermometer fell to 40° Fahr. Next day brought them a lovely morning, and, at two p.m., they set out for the spring, to which, as he was the discoverer, Mr. Mann's name was given. They found a little runnel of pure cold water, issuing from peaty earth, embowered in blue flowers, and surrounded by nettles. Here the camp was fixed, and for five weeks it became the base of their researches and the centre of their excursions. It was 7,000 feet above the sea, and was held by common consent to be an admirable spot for a sanatorium or a colony. Materials for roads or for house-building lay around in abundance, and, in his enthusiasm, Captain Burton exclaimed, "Where can a Lebanon be found equal to the beautiful, the majestic Cameroons?" "Here," says Mr. Saker, in a lower key, "we had a glorious sky, a dry air, in fact an English home, and no great obstacles in the ascent but what a little patient toil will overcome."

Christmas-eve and Christmas-day were spent in taking bearings, rambling about the hills, and in naming places. The main peak they discovered to be divided into a pair of distinct heads, which they christened Victoria and Albert. "Little did we think," remarks Mr. Saker, "that the nation and our beloved Sovereign were then being plunged into irreparable grief by Prince Albert's death." Another summit was named Earthwork Crater, and the elevation near which they were encamped, Mount Helen, after Mrs. Saker, who had supplied the Christmas pudding. From its cone there was a wonderful prospect of wild scenery and of perplexing confusion. Twenty-eight deep crevasses were counted, with numberless thick lava beds and ribs of scoriaceous rock. The morning of Christmas-day was spent by Mr. Saker, in company with Captain Burton, in a climb to the summit of Earthwork Crater, about thirteen miles from Victoria, and five from the main peak of the mountain. The volcano had apparently long burnt itself out, and the pools of water formed during the rains at the bottom of the crater were the resort of the small birds that abound in its vicinity. Returning from this excursion, and breakfast despatched, Mr. Saker left the party, and descended the mountain for Cameroons, where some important duties required his attention. Early in January, however, in company with his colleague in the Mission, Mr. Smith, he rejoined the mountaineers. They had passed the time in exploring a portion of the higher regions, but were suffering from exposure and fatigue. Mr. Smith being too unwell to go farther, Mr. Saker, with some Kroo boys, on the 13th, left the camp to climb Victoria, the highest of the twin peaks. The ascent was made on the south side.

" During my absence," writes Mr. Saker, " Mr. Mann
had ascended the north side, while Consul Burton
attempted the south face. After a day's weary toil over
beds of lava, we reached the foot of a small mount
somewhat sheltering to weary travellers. There I spread
my blanket and passed the night. It was a glorious
evening, but somewhat cold. At early dawn I found
the glass at 31° Fahr. But the sun rose, a cloudless
morning, and it soon grew warm. At six I began
the ascent, and at ten reached the southern summit
or ridge. By this time it was very warm, and the wind
that sweeps so fearfully in these regions seemed hushed.
Light fleecy clouds ever and anon shut in the surrounding scenery. Towards the east I saw a range of
mountains that I had never before observed, and took
its bearings; but the attempt to secure the angles of
summits towards the west was not so successful. Ere
I could bring two points together, one would be ob-
scured.

"At this highest point I found the water boil at
188°, thermometer 58°. This gives an elevation nearly
the same as our charts, the result of trigonometrical
survey below. My attempt to explore the Crater was
a failure. The whole was enshrouded in cloud. The
Crater must be of enormous extent. Its two peaks
present a large angle at seven miles distance. After a
long delay, I began the descent, and at two reached
my last night's resting-place. After rest and refreshment,
we set out on return to our camp. Here I found the
Consul a little better, but still unable to walk much.
As I had stayed on this second run up the mountain
ten days, I was now compelled to leave for Victoria and
Cameroons. We have ascertained that there are native

8*

towns at about 3,500 feet elevation, that cultivation extends but little farther, and that beyond these heights there is every inducement to seek a temporary home for invalids and wearied missionaries."

A final ascent was made by Captain Burton and his companions on the 27th of January. In this Mr. Saker did not participate, as he had returned to Amboises Bay. The investigators encountered intense cold. Their waterproof coats were white with hoar-frost, and the summit was powdered with frozen dew. Before leaving the peak, Captain Burton was able to discover a complete solfaterra, lying to the north-east of Albert Crater. Smoke arose in puffy volumes from long lines of white marl and sulphur. This discovery accounts for the many detached reports of flames seen issuing from the mountain by the merchants of Cameroons and the people of Fernando Po. It would seem, therefore, that the great volcanic mountain of Cameroons is not yet an extinct volcano. A hailstorm signalised the descent. "Finally," adds Consul Burton, "on the 2nd of February, 1862, I once more saw the scattered bungalows of Victoria, where the kindly Mrs. Saker, who would not leave the place till our safe return, received me with all hospitality."*

---

* For the materials of this chapter, besides Mr. Saker's letters, I am indebted to the Report presented to the Foreign Office by Consul Burton, and kindly forwarded to the Mission House by Lord Russell. It is also printed in the " Proceedings of the Royal Geographical Society," vol. vi., p. 238.

CHAPTER XII.

In Perils on Every Side, 1862—1863.

THE next eighteen months of Mr. Saker's missionary life were months of unceasing toil and constant anxiety. His expectations with regard to the early colonising of Amboises Bay were only partially fulfilled. The English Government hesitated to avail themselves of the advantages which it presented as a coaling station, and a healthful resort for the sick crews of the men-of-war on the coast. Clarence Cove continued to be the head-quarters of the squadron, and trade naturally remained in its former channels. The people were, therefore, disinclined to leave the place where their property and livelihood were secure. There were, however, some compensations for the slow development of the colony. The government of it could be more easily controlled; time was allowed for the foundation of the town, and its due supply with the necessaries and conveniences of life. At the commencement of 1862, eighty-two persons had settled there, of whom one-half were children connected with the families of the converts, and a portion of whom came from Fernando Po to be educated under the care of Mr. Pinnock, the resident pastor of the church. Some fifty or sixty persons habitually attended public worship, a few of them natives from the mountains. Mr. Saker thus

refers to them in a letter to Lady Peto:—"You will be pleased to hear that some of the poor dark natives near this place are not only listening to the Gospel when taken to their towns, but are attending the services in our little chapel. Many who never heard the name of Jesus are listening to the offers of salvation through a crucified Saviour. It is not unusual to hear them exclaim aloud or talk to each other on the subject to which they are listening."

The Rev. R. Smith, on visiting Victoria, thus describes his impressions of the place:—"It is a delightsome spot, very beautiful for situation. The little town appears to be rising very slowly. There are several good houses already built on the estate, and a vast number of people live on the mountains around. I made a journey to one of the fishing towns some distance off, in company with our esteemed and loved brother Johnson. After we had climbed over the rocks, and journeyed through the bush three parts of the way, a light tornado overtook us, and wetted us a little. We pressed on to the town close by, and were well repaid for anything we suffered. We had a good meeting in King George's house, the people listening attentively to the good news. The King's 'palace' consisted of one large room, with a few feet partitioned off for a bed-room, a mud floor, three or four stands for drying fish, with wood fires underneath. There were as many drying tables as the King has wives. A number of black earthen pots for cooking completed the utensils in the room. I counted seven goats that live and sleep in the house, and a pig is no uncommon member of the family circle. Three wives and a number of children made up the household present on our visit."

VICTORIA CHAPEL, AMBOISES BAY.

Such is a fair specimen of the best of the houses of the Bakwili, among whom the missionaries were labouring to introduce the Gospel with its elevating tendencies and hopes.

At Cameroons, Mr. Saker was made intensely sorrowful by the increasing ill-health of his wife and daughter. In August he was obliged to part with them. The loss this was to his work the following extracts from his letter of August 29th (1862) will show :—" To-day, I send away to England my wife, daughter, and servant. These, one and all, are worn down to a low, low condition physically, but their flow of spirits seems unconquerable. Of Mrs. S. I say not a word here ; but it seems right that I give a line of information of the others, but chiefly of my daughter. Soon after her arrival here, I pointed out a line of labour which I wished her to undertake, but, after looking round, she saw so much work to be done in other ways that she decided for herself what to do. Of course, in the presence of so much work, I could only consent; yet did I inwardly say, 'The novelty will soon wear off, and then she will weary of it.' But it has not been so. She has maintained her plans till now. She chose the day-school, and has continued it with much diligence till a week since. She found the women of the church in much ignorance and wishing for help. She attempted their improvement by opening a service in the town, at the house of one of the members, for women only, devoting the afternoon of one day in the week to this, and meeting the same body of women on the Sabbath-day, instead of attending the Sabbath-school. Although these meetings have all been more or less religious services, reading and expounding Scripture and prayer, at first using our excellent friend the owner

of the house as interpreter, but latterly doing without
him, often have I detected her composing sermons
for the Sabbath. Thus has she done much to gladden
and instruct these poor women, and they grieve for her
leaving. She has also devoted one afternoon in the
week to teaching them needlework. Of Maria, I can
only say she has been a right hand to Mrs. Saker, and
heart and soul one with her. To her and Eliza I am
indebted for stitching all our books as the first step in
binding. This has mostly been the work of evenings."

Pleasant, indeed, is this sight of the entire family of
our missionary brother giving itself to the work of God ;
combining together, each in their measure, to impart the
knowledge of both temporal and spiritual things to the
ignorant and degraded children of Africa.

The task was no easy one. Often was it interrupted
by bad health ; by violent disputes among the people ;
by the outbreak of war ; and by the vile attempts of
white men to revive the abolished trade in slaves. Thus,
under date of September 20th (1862), Mr. Saker writes :
"After Mrs. S. left me on the 30th ultimo, I came
home only to lie down and sicken, and suffered a sharp
attack for five days. I then recovered. During that
same time Smith, too, was suffering daily from repeated
fevers." Again, in the same letter : "Just now we are
living in perpetual and daily quarrelling. There seems
but little business going on at present, and the natives
take advantage of the leisure to exhaust themselves
in wrangling and fierce disputes. Three times this
month have I been called home to prevent open
war. To-day—nearly half a day spent in quelling an
enraged multitude. The steam is blown off now ; but
only to be renewed on Monday." Nature, too, seemed

often unpropitious. "A fearful storm of rain came on us on Wednesday night last. It commenced just a little before eight, while our classes were still in chapel, and abated not till after twelve. Then again at three in the morning, and lasted for half an hour, accompanied with wind, lightning, and thunder. Our people could not go home from meeting till past midnight." In seven hours, by his rain gauge, Mr. Saker found that seven and a-half inches of rain had fallen. The damage done to the Mission buildings was great, and required many weeks to repair.

Here is another scene of savage life, and of the part played in it by the missionary:—"Saturday night, late, the principal chief of A'kwa town came home, and heard all one side of the dispute. He allowed himself to be excited to madness. At four in the morning he beat his drum, calling all out to war. At five our yard and outbuildings were filled with women and children of the weaker party. At six the small town close to us was invaded by a hostile multitude. We counselled quietness, and took resistance into our own hands. By this means we prevented much bloodshed, and saved most of the property. Smith and Fuller resisted these demoniacal men manfully, and by nine we had so far succeeded in quieting the rabble that we saw the last of them out of the town. The destruction of hundreds of plantain and fruit trees makes a desolate show; but this, and the breaking down of four or five houses, is the chief damage. So our Sabbath was broken up; but we had a good and quiet meeting in the afternoon and evening."

The resistance alluded to above was that of earnest and fearless remonstrance. From the first Mr. Saker rejected the use of any weapon for self-defence. Amidst all the perils he encountered in the wilderness from the rage of man he never resorted to violence or retaliation for his protection. He was strong in meekness, in patience, and in imperturbable quietness of spirit, and in his calm trust in God.

Later in the year, two slaves belonging to Portuguese owners on the coast, having escaped, found their way to the Cameroons river. They were claimed by a trader, who sold the man and kept the woman for a worse purpose. Escaping again, they were befriended by Mr. Saker. From this arose another attack on the mission-house by the trader's slaves, and for some days the lives of the missionaries were in serious danger. The poor refugees at length found a place of security at Victoria.

But, in spite of all these agitations and sore besetments, the Word of God was not bound. Writing at the close of the year (December 27, 1862) this unresting toiler reports :—" God has graciously given us an increase to our church. You will remember that our last increase was in August, the last Sabbath in the month, that Mrs. S. and Eliza might participate in our joy. On that occasion our brother Smith baptized; and now to-day five others are given to us, and to-morrow, being the last Sabbath of the year, they are to be baptized. Mr. Fuller will have the pleasure of leading these lowly ones into our river. Very many things conspire to make this increase joyous to me, and not the least of these that one more from out of our own family is called to God, and is honoured by His grace. It is a special mercy to us, that our hearts be not too much oppressed nor cast down."

The severe strain of these events on Mr. Saker's health again raised the question of the necessity of his seeking an invigorating clime. For more than twenty years he had borne, with a resolution of mind and will that few men could be found to exercise, the debilitating **diseases** of this pestilential coast. He had seen one after another of **his** colleagues and companions yield **to their** deadly assaults. Himself with an emaciated frame and a shaken constitution, he yet persisted in his work. " I cannot hope," he writes on the 31st of March, 1863, " to live much longer in Africa. The weakness and suffering of the past month have convinced me that if **my life is** to be preserved I **must** journey to you." Although he sometimes regarded his life as useless—for his preaching, he said, was curtailed to the lowest point—he could not contemplate an abandonment of the work without the deepest repugnance and **sorrow.** But from the opening of the year it seemed his imperative duty to leave. Circumstances at home had also rendered it important that he should again see the Committee. The attacks on his methods of operation, alluded to in a previous chapter, had been renewed, and unfortunately received a certain measure of support from some who were not wholly unacquainted with the exigencies of an African clime, and the perils of a pioneering life among savage races of men. A request, therefore, came from head-quarters that he would revisit his native land. In his uncertainty of the future, he replied to the Secretary's letter conveying the wish of the Committee : "I shall obey your summons as soon as I can. Certainly I cannot leave before the 28th Feb. (1863), and then my foolish heart asks, Who is to care for this land ? But this is weakness, if not worse

The cause is God's, and if He calls me away He can take care of it, either by me or by some other means. Only let me see my duty in the matter, and then reason and command both say, 'Go forward.' The God of all grace comfort your heart with strong hope and faith."

He felt it, however, necessary that he should remain, if possible, till the return of the Rev. R. Smith, who was then on a brief visit to England. This took place on the 29th of May, and early in July Mr. Saker once more left his work. It is needless to encumber these pages with controversies which are now forgotten, but which at the time were productive of much personal distress. He was heartily welcomed by all who knew his worth and the nobleness of his character, and not less cordially did the Committee, after " full investigation," give expression to their satisfaction "at the diligence, the zeal, the self-denial, and the success" with which he had planted the Christian faith in new fields, on a barbarous coast, amidst wild uncultured tribes, and founded "a Christian colony whence civilisation and the Gospel may spread; " and all achieved " in the midst of perils by sea and land, among savages thirsting for his blood, or by their spells hoping to destroy his life."

CHAPTER XIII.

MR. SAKER was much refreshed and invigorated by his year's sojourn in England, and by the Christian intercourse he enjoyed in the numerous deputation visits he paid to the churches. On the 21st of September, 1864, a deeply interesting farewell service was held in Bloomsbury Chapel, at which the Rev. Q. W. Thomson was also set apart for the service of Christ in Africa. With Mrs. Saker and her three daughters, the two missionaries went on board the mail steamer at Liverpool on the following Saturday. On the 1st of October Mr. Saker writes from Madeira to the Rev. F. Trestrail:—"We are quietly at anchor here. Our passage has been one of some discomfort, but of much mercy, and we are all in health and looking forward to our future run as one of peace and pleasure. We left Liverpool with fine weather, which continued all the Sabbath, and we enjoyed an hour's public worship in the saloon. On Monday the wind increased, making it difficult to move about. It was worse on Tuesday. On Wednesday it increased to a strong gale. Thursday morning it moderated, and continued improving to last evening, when we all assembled on deck. At midnight we made the island, and came to anchor at daylight. We are now

anticipating a day's enjoyment on shore with our friends.
Affectionate remembrances from Mrs. S. and our girls;
also from Mr. Thomson." From this point to Sierra
Leone the voyage was most pleasant, and, calling at
several ports on the way, intercourse was enjoyed with
many Christian friends. Writing on the 13th of October
from Sierra Leone, Mr. Saker says :—" The few hours at
that lovely place, Madeira, will not soon be forgotten.
We had a short run on shore at Teneriffe, but the rain
made it unpleasant. At Gambia we spent a few hours
with the good Wesleyan brother who is there labouring
faithfully, but whose health is fast failing. And now
here also are we tasting the joy of Christian society.
At Madeira it was with the Presbyterians; at Gambia,
with Wesleyans; and here, with Episcopalians. And
yet, in all, spiritual life is the same, and, but for some
external manifestations that are apart from Christian
life, it would be very difficult to point to differences.
How glorious, how precious, is this *oneness* of life in
Christ. May the day soon dawn when the Saviour's
prayer may be fulfilled—'that they all may be one.'"

The last fourteen days of the voyage were not so
pleasant as the earlier portion of it. Many days were
wet, and the rains continued for some days after their
arrival at Cameroons, which took place on the 29th
of October. " I am very thankful," says Mr. Saker, in
conclusion, "that we are all preserved and brought
safely to our distant home, and that we meet our
brethren, our friends, and our (school) children in so
much health and comfort. May this, our re-union, be
greatly promotive of *good* to this country, to each other,
and also glorifying to our God."

There was no delay in recommencing his interrupted

labours, and in a few weeks we find Mr. Saker reporting that he had laid the foundation of a new brick chapel at Bethel, that his translation of the Old Testament had been resumed, and Ruth, Nahum, Habakkuk, and Zephaniah, for school purposes, were in the press. The services at all the stations were revived with fresh vigour. His new iron boat had been put together, and was already employed in communicating with Victoria and in visiting the outlying tribes among which evangelistic efforts had been or were about to be commenced. Briefly, he announces that Mr. Pinnock had had the joy of baptizing two converts. "The attendance at Hickory is excellent. At John A'kwa's Town, Mr. Fuller's new home, very bad. Here at Bethel we are crowded. At Mr. Pinnock's place we can sometimes get a few. At Bell's Town a good company. We wish for, we pray for, and expect a large increase. Pray for us that the blessing may come."

Sickness and death soon, however, began to enter the small circle of devoted labourers. The wife of Mr. Smith fell a prey to disease on the 27th of January (1865), after a brief life of Christian toil; while Mr. Thomson and the younger members of Mr. Saker's family were often down with constantly recurring fevers. Death also bore away some of the best of the early converts, who died witnessing in death, as in life, the power of the Gospel to win the most debased of mankind to holiness, and fit them for the bliss of a better land.

Thus, under sunshine and cloud, in weariness often, disease ever haunting his steps, in the midst of dangers that no human foresight could avert, this heroic man pursued the one great aim of his life. It were a repetition of the like actions and the same devotedness, to follow Mr. Saker through the next four years in which he was permitted to pursue his course. Frequent spells of bodily suffering did not prevent the achievement of the objects on which his heart was set. War for a time might disturb the quiet progress of his work; his helpers might fail, or the necessary material for the needed buildings might be long in coming to hand; still, with unremitting vigour, the work was carried on. Chapels and school-houses and mission-houses, at Bethel, at Victoria, at Hickory, and at Bell Town, were planned and made; repairs of buildings, falling into constant decay from the ravages of insects or of storms, were made; and, above all, the care of the churches, the training of the young, the translation of the Scriptures, the preparation of vocabularies and school books, and the exercise of an influence deservedly won in the counsels of the tribes, and which was ever used for the preservation of peace, civilisation, and good government;—all, and every one of these various departments of missionary labour received Mr. Saker's incessant attention, and called forth the energies of his ever active mind. Exhausting and depressing as is the climate of this region of Africa, Mr. Saker filled every hour with some needed work.

In his letters, Mr. Saker seldom enters into much detail. For the most part he describes his employments in a few short, pithy sentences. He was too busy to give the time to composition, or to dwell on the special features of his work. A few excerpts from his papers will sufficiently exhibit the variety of his aims, and his mode of working.

Thus, on the 31st of March (1866) he says:—" The month closes heavily on us. For two weeks we have

CHAPEL AT HICKORY TOWN, CAMEROONS.

been in the midst of war and its consequences, and no
hope of peace yet. Our work, our journeys, our meetings are all more or less impeded. We have to-day our
usual service, and to-morrow we hope to have meetings
in all the hostile towns. Isaiah is finished. This week
I begin a new work. Our chapel will have been quite
silent this month. The men have been compelled to
take the musket and sword instead of the trowel. Our
friend Johnson has gone at last, and his family are in
deep sorrow."

Mr. Horton Johnson was Mr. Saker's first convert,
and became, under his instruction, one of the most
useful and efficient servants of the Mission. His piety
and zeal were conspicuous, and his loss was most
severely felt by Mr. Saker and the native church.

Another month Mr. Saker writes: "Our brethren
have taken advantage of the fine weather, and have been
journeying. This has left me all the work of the station,
besides much translation, printing, and building ; sixteen hours daily, with scarcely time to eat. It will be
pleasant for you to know that I have gone on all the
month without suffering from it, and am now strong for
another month of toil. Our war here is not at an end,
but may break out at any moment. The madness and
savagery of both sides are a sad interruption to us.
But what are our disputes, and hatred, and slaughter
to that of the European Continent [the Franco-German
War]! True, both are alike desperate, both are the
result of ambition ; but there they separate—they only
unite in the character of the misery it entails. Oh !
when will the Kingdom of Peace be set up ?"

Again he writes in July, 1866: "As to our success
in our toils I cannot say much. I have just finished

9

Matthew, almost a new translation, as every verse and
every word has been revised, and the best possible
representation given to the Greek as far as I can do it.
Indeed, the present edition is doubtless my final attempt
to give the people the true Word of Life. Some ten
years have passed since the Matthew we use was printed;
during that time my knowledge of the language has
been steadily increasing. I can give a better rendering
now than I could then. Some five chapters of Mark
are now in the press, and I shall this month print as
far as my paper will allow. While this new revision
of the Gospels is going through the press, other parts
of the Old Testament are to keep pace with it. I am
busy now with the Book of Job. While I await paper
from you I must attend to Mr. Thomson's dwelling.
Certain buildings must be had. For instance, all the
cooking must be done out of the house. Then there
are sheds for goats, fowls, &c.; all adds to the expense.
We are looking forward to a small addition to our
church next month; it may be six weeks. There are
only two accepted at present."

Mr. Saker's frequent journeys to Victoria often ex-
posed him to great danger. On one occasion he had a
narrow escape from being drowned. A sudden rush of
wind swayed the boom of his little schooner, and he was
swept into the sea. By the help of the boatmen he was
quickly rescued, but had to sit for eight hours in his wet
clothes.

The steady and continuous growth of his work
more than compensated him for all his toil and sufferings. The work of the Lord prospered under his hand.
In his last letter of the year 1868 he had the joy to
announce the virtual completion of the version of the

Old Testament scriptures. "The year's toil is over," he writes. "Through God's manifold mercy I have completed the translation of the entire Bible, with the exception of a few chapters of Chronicles, which are so nearly like parts of the Books of Kings that I omitted them till other books were finished. Those chapters I shall not write till next rains, as in the months of January and February I must be out in the country and towns adjacent. You are aware that, after my recovery in February last, I sought to print the revised 'Acts of the Apostles,' and then the Psalms. This done, my health emboldened me to resolve on the translation of all the remaining books of the Old Testament, and I am exceedingly thankful that God has helped me to go through it, although I have suspended nearly everything else, except the preaching, for this one work. Some books have given me great trouble. There are constructions in Ezekiel which I cannot even now understand sufficiently to render into intelligible sentences ; even the English rendering I do not understand. If a few things in the 'Acts' wearied my brain for hours, Ezekiel has held me for days. Some of his words I must read and read again ere I can print.

"Our church increases slowly. We baptized six ; three others are accepted, and two from Dido Town, the reward of the faithful toil of N'Kwe, and where also Mr. Smith has often visited. These will be baptized in a few days. Our congregation increases slowly too. Sometimes we feel oppressed at the few who will hear ; at other times nearly a full house of earnest hearers fills one with joy and hope."

Early in the year 1869 Mr. Saker again resolved on a visit to England. His colleagues had all of them, in the

three or four years previous, been compelled to return
home for invigoration and health ; and Mrs. Saker and
her children had been absent for many months. Events
to be presently referred to also rendered it expedient
that he should confer with the Committee. For twenty-
five years he had laboured in the tropics, and, although
his indomitable spirit forbade him to relinquish the
task, it was yet doubtful whether his strength would
permit or justify a prolongation of that intense devotion which had so wonderfully and so long sustained
him. Leaving, therefore, his colleagues, now well inured
to the work, he tore himself away, and in the month
of May once more reached his native land, emaciated,
pale, feeble, and deeply suffering, yet ready at a moment's
call to risk all for Christ and or the souls of men.

CHAPTER XIV.

WENTY-FOUR years had more than elapsed since Mr. Saker commenced his missionary life among the Dualla towns on the River Cameroons. Brief visits had been paid to them by Dr. Prince and Mr. Clarke in the early years of the Mission; but Mr. Saker was the first missionary to settle there. His first dwelling, as we have seen, was a native hut, without windows or outlet, except the door, raised on a mound of earth, the walls formed of split bamboo, and plaited palm leaves for the roof. The people were utterly barbarous, without knowledge or written language, without clothing except of the rudest and most meagre kind, unacquainted with the arts of social life, or with the customs of civilised society, except such as ministered rather to their degradation, and the indulgence of vicious inclinations. Food fit for Europeans was nearly unattainable, and the cultivation practised by the people was so scanty and wretched as to leave them for a large part of the year dependent on the spontaneous fruits of the ground. Communication with England was unfrequent, and Mr. Saker and his family were more than once on the verge of starvation.

Unaided, except by his devoted wife and a native

convert or two from Clarence, Mr. Saker had alone, in the first instance, to grapple with these difficulties. A better house, if only for health's sake, had to be erected. The first buildings were necessarily of wood, and it was the perishable nature of this material that led Mr. Saker subsequently to attempt the manufacture of bricks. By degrees, the converts and others of the people were taught the use of the hammer, the chisel, and the plane; the moulded clay was burnt, and a house of enduring materials was built. Gradually and slowly the permanent buildings in which the work of the Mission was carried on were constructed from Mr. Saker's designs, and erected under his incessant supervision.

But this went on not at one station only. At Dido's Town, at Bell Town, at John A'kwa's Town, at Hickory or Mortonville, more or less of this beneficent work was accomplished; and, last of all, a permanent township with its laws and regulations was established on Amboises Bay; a mission chapel and residence for the missionary were erected, and assistance was given to the colonists to establish themselves in their new home, where freedom to worship God and perfect liberty were to the fullest extent secured and enjoyed.

But if the achievement of these varied results absorbed a great deal of time, we have seen that the more direct duties of a missionary's life were not neglected. Every available moment was consecrated to the acquisition of the language, in reducing it to a written form, and in the employment of the press to furnish the people with the Scriptures and other useful books. Many days and weeks were spent in itineracy, in order that the knowledge of the Gospel might be given to the

tribes dwelling on the higher reaches of the river, and
yet farther into the interior : while the fruits of his
earnest ministry at the stations were gathered into
schools and congregations. All had to be effected in
spite of frequent sickness and necessary absences, the
hostility of some of the tribes, and the wearing away
of both physical and mental energies in the miasmatic
atmosphere of the deadly Western Coast of Africa. One
missionary after another had come and gone, some to
the rest of God, others driven away by the fatalities
that await all who sojourn there.

At the time of which we now write (1869) there remained, of all the devoted men who had consecrated their
lives to the Mission besides Mr. Saker, only the two young
brethren, Mr. Robert Smith and Mr. Q. W. Thomson
from England, and Mr. Joseph Fuller and Mr. Pinnock
from Jamaica.   To the deep distress of Mr. Saker, there
had arisen during the last few years much diversity of
judgment between him and them, and which for a short
time seemed to threaten the existence of the Mission
itself. Correspondence and forbearance had alike failed
to restore harmony. At length, the Committee of the
Society deemed it necessary, once for all, to make an
investigation upon the spot into the alleged grounds of
complaint. For this purpose, in the autumn of the
year, the Committee requested me to accompany Mr.
and Mrs. Saker on their return.

Accordingly, with my beloved wife, and in the company of Mr. and Mrs. Saker and their daughter Emily,
I sailed from Liverpool in the steamship *Athenian*.
The first two days of the voyage were stormy, but the
clouds dispersed, and the rest of the way the sea was
calm and the journey uneventful. We landed at Bethel

Station, King A'kwa's town, on the 7th of December, in health and safety. During the month that I was permitted to remain, my time was wholly occupied with the questions that had brought me to Cameroons, and I had but few opportunities for journeying beyond the area occupied by the brethren in their daily toil. I was very soon convinced that the alienation of feeling and contrariety of action, which were soon made painfully apparent to me, sprang chiefly, if not altogether, from a diversity of judgment as to the conduct of the Mission. The younger brethren were of opinion that, while a certain amount of secular work in putting up buildings and keeping them in repair was requisite, too much time and attention had been given to them by Mr. Saker, to the detriment of the more spiritual part of the work. By an unfortunate concurrence of circumstances, these differences had acquired an importance altogether unanticipated. In 1863 the home Committee had given power to a local Committee of all the missionaries on the spot to meet, as often as might seem desirable, to discuss and decide, subject to their approval, all questions of interest, both secular and religious, affecting the welfare of the Mission. This arrangement came into operation in 1864, but, before the end of that year, the removal of all the senior brethren by death, or from other causes, had left the management of these matters in the hands of the younger men mentioned above.*

Mr. Saker soon found himself alone and unsupported in the councils of this Committee. It is unnecessary to enter into any minute detail of the events that followed.

* Mr. Thomson only arrived in Africa at the end of the year 1864.

It was, to say the least, unfortunate. The discussions that arose, and the resistance he met with, gave intense pain to the senior member of the Committee, and after a short time he withdrew from its deliberations, continuing to pursue the course which the home Committee, on a previous occasion, had declared to be "necessary to the well-being of the Mission." It can surprise no one that Mr. Saker should decline to allow his actions to be judged, and his views of what was necessary for "the well-being of the Mission" to be canvassed, in an adverse sense, by brethren who were so much his juniors in age, in experience, in knowledge of missionary affairs, and in acquaintance with the people. They were zealous, assiduous in the discharge of the duties they had undertaken, but had only a limited acquaintance with the severe toil which had secured the advantages they now enjoyed. Mr. Saker, too, was by natural constitution reserved in speech, apt to be silent when resisted, and to retire into himself when no readiness was shown to accept his conclusions, or to act with him in furtherance of his plans. Nor could he tolerate any lack of industry or zeal. Ever himself fighting against the debilitating effects of the climate, he did not, perhaps, make sufficient allowance for weaker natures that, as he thought, too easily succumbed to their power.

It is due to Mr. Saker that his views on the subject referred to should be given. Writing to me in June, 1870, he says:—" As to secular work, what is it if rightly looked at? That which I have done I look at as a portion of my highest honour. In all mechanical knowledge, I have not had to give a moment's study; and what is it to me if I find a nation in utter ignorance of all common arts? I point out to them a better way of labour, a word here, a five minutes' handling of tool there—all this is far less than what others have given to idle gossip. Then, on buildings for the Mission; where would we all have been if still confined to the frail, sickly huts of the heathen? Deaths among us have diminished in proportion to a better housing, and how can we get better houses but by personal labour? persevering labour, and with a double object—to secure a healthy dwelling, with instruction to the natives, young and old, to go and do likewise. This, it is said, is all very well, but it has been to the neglect of the work of a missionary. *That* means spiritual work, as they would express it. With such, the true work of the missionary is, it seems, to go, book in hand, under a tree here and a shed there, and preach to the people. With me the work has ever appeared in a different light. It is to go to the man in his house, to sympathise in his sorrows and cares, to aid him to *think* of a better condition and of the means to attain it. Then, when his attention has been gained, to speak of that higher life which we have lost, and which the loving hand of God will give us again, if we will hear Him.

"Who, my dear brother, is to measure the value of such a simple lesson given from one heart to another heart, from a soul in light to a soul in darkness? And what if such a lesson be given by showing a better way of planting and building? I know that this method has no *éclat*: there is no noise, but I know there are great results. In all places where God has permitted me to labour, the first efforts have in part passed away, but now we can get a settled congregation. Yet, while there are heathen around us, the work must go on from house to house, and from heart to heart, if it is to succeed. To me it has ever been that the spiritual work is to get at the heart of the individual man. How it is done I don't care a pin. The Master wrought so; the apostles in their various modes so worked, but still using the public assemblies when they could, as on the Mount, in an upper room, on Mar's Hill, or by the waterbrook, where prayer was often offered."

All must feel that is a sufficient and forcible vindication of Mr. Saker's methods of operation. It needs no comment. It is complete, and requires no further explanation.

But, in connection with Mr. Saker's secular labours, it was also affirmed that there had been much waste, and even extravagance. With regard to this point, I may be permitted to quote the observations I addressed to the Committee :—"Doubtless some mistakes have been made, as was inevitable through the novelty of the circumstances. Experiments were tried which could not have been done without expense. Some instances were mentioned to me which were evidently nothing more than differences of judgment between Mr. Saker and the local board; the latter judging that to be wasteful which did not meet with their approval. But it must be remembered that Mr. Saker found nothing to his hand; he had to plan, to conceive, to construct everything, with few or no resources on the spot. After the fullest consideration I could give to these adverse statements, and after inspecting the presumed evidences of this waste, it is my deliberate judgment that, while in some cases the statements have been exaggerations, in others, when the destructive effects of climate are considered, the interruptions occasioned by illness, the thefts of the native population, the slow and inadequate workmanship of the men Mr. Saker has had to instruct, the delay arising from want of materials to finish the work, and for which resort must be had to the stores and workshops of England, Mr. Saker has done his best, has never wilfully wasted the Society's property, and has not been guilty of extravagance. On the contrary, I marvel at the amount of work, both secular and religious, accomplished in the twenty-four years of Mr. Saker's toil. He has exhibited an endurance, a devotedness in the Master's service, an heroic struggle with perils and difficulties on every hand, which few missionaries are called to exercise, and which his successors will not have to encounter. I should be unfaithful to my convictions if I were not anew to commend Mr. Saker to the fullest confidence of the Committee, or to speak of him as among the greatest of modern missionaries of the Cross."

During my stay I was able to visit all the stations occupied by the brethren. My last visit, in the company of my dear wife and Mr. Saker, was to Victoria. Two days were occupied in the voyage there and back, in an open boat, protected by an awning from the scorching sun. The crew consisted of four Cameroons men (Christians) and four Kroo boys. It was early morning when we started, and, the moon being near her full, it was very light. Partly rowing and partly under sail, about eight o'clock we entered one of the creeks which unite the Cameroons and Bimbia rivers. It was a beautiful pull among the mangrove-trees which grew in profusion at the water's edge, while the Bimbia mountains, which constitute the lower ranges of the great Cameroons mountain, added grandeur to the scene. The necessity of reaching Amboises Bay by daylight would not allow us when passing Bimbia to seek an interview with King William, whose house stands on an eminence a short distance from the river. Leaving the river for the sea, we weathered two or three promontories, and crossed the mouth of Man-of-War Bay. The coast scenery was very fine. It was rocky, consisting of masses of basalt and trap, covered with fine timber to the water's edge, where the sea broke in wild surf. The shore-hills were backed by lofty mountains, and could we have seen the great peak, which obstinately clothed itself with clouds and fog during nearly the whole time of our stay, the scenery would have exhibited its grandest and noblest forms. We caught the faintest glimmer of the mountain's shape and magnitude, only sufficient to intensify our disappointment. About four o'clock we rounded the island of Mandoleh, at the entrance of Amboises Bay, and Victoria lay before us on its little clearing, and its few houses scattered along the shore. Mr. Saker pointed out to us the chapel, Mr. Pinnock's house, Mr. Wilson's, and other cottages erected by the people. These friends came down to the beach to receive us, as the surf drove our boat on shore amidst the sprinkling of the spray.

Mr. Pinnock's house became our home during our brief stay. We found the colony to consist of some 200 persons, all of whom were under the efficient instruction of Mr. Pinnock; either in the day-school, which he personally taught, or in his Bible-class and Sunday-school, or in the sanctuary. A few of the mountain people had lately settled in the town, and a village had been formed, about a mile from Victoria, of the fishing population inhabiting the islands of the bay. Here a school-house had been built and the village was regularly visited by the pastor or some of his members. Most of the houses of the nascent colony were well-built of timber, and some progress had been made in boat-building. I saw a schooner of considerable size on the stocks, nearly ready for launching. Frequent intercourse was kept up with Fernando Po, where the produce of the colonists found a ready market, and from whence children of former members of the church came to the school under Mr. Pinnock's care. I was greatly pleased with the neatness of the people, their industry, their love for their minister and for the house of God. Two days were passed in pleasant intercourse with the people, and we left with regret this fair scene of hopeful toil.

On the morning of the day following our return to Bethel, my dear wife was suddenly called away to her heavenly home. The exposure of the previous days and the great heat brought on an apoplectic attack, which, without any warning, robbed me of her sweet companionship. The prostration which followed her decease, and the fever which seized me during the first days of January, prevented the fulfilment of my intention to make several excursions into the interior. But the main object of my visit was accomplished, and I had the pleasure of seeing relations of friendship and co-operation re-established and harmony restored.

This chapter will be best closed with a few extracts from the report which I presented to the Committee. "It is with more than pleasure that I state that *all* the brethren sustain cheerfully the hardships which this work entails, and endure with manly and Christian patience personal sufferings which fall to the lot of few missionaries in any part of the mission field.

For the Lord's sake, for the sake of the salvation of these savage and barbarous tribes, they gladly encounter numerous perils, and fearlessly meet the dangers which a residence among uncivilised people involves. They are worthy of the churches that sent them forth, and of the support rendered them by the Society whose missionaries they are.

"The effect of these various labours in King A'kwa's town is very visible, not only in the improved dwellings which are springing up, and in the introduction of the customs of civilised life among the people, but in the abolition of the sanguinary practices which formerly prevailed; in the evident decay of superstition; in the influence of the missionary in the counsels of the chiefs; in the numbers who attend the house of God; in the estimation in which the missionary and the converts are generally held; and in the desire of the people for instruction.

"The tribes living on the higher reaches of the river, as well as others nearer to the sea, are quite ready to welcome a missionary to reside among them. The only thing that hinders is the miserable jealousy of the tribes among whom our brethren now labour, who fear that the residence of a missionary in these inner regions would in some way injure their monopoly of the trade, which is every day increasing in importance; and in these foolish ideas they are encouraged, I am sorry to say, by some of the European traders who frequent the river. On more than one occasion force has been used by the natives to prevent the missionary from settling among other tribes; but it may be hoped that their prejudices will ere long be removed, or that our brethren may be able to seize some favourable opportunity to fulfil the wishes of these more distant people, though it may for a time involve an entire separation from the stations now occupied.

" It now only remains that I should record in the warmest terms my thankfulness for the welcome which my beloved wife and myself received from the brethren and their partners, their readiness to supply me with the information I required, the solicitude displayed by all, and especially by Mr. and Mrs. Saker, with whom I took up my residence, for our comfort and health, and, above all, for the tender sympathy shown me by the brethren in the great sorrow that befell me. If I left in Africa with irrepressible grief the remains of one most dear to me, my companion and helper in all my travels in the service of the Society, I have nevertheless come away with feelings of gratitude to God for the work which His servants have wrought, and for the success which He has graciously given them. The African Mission abundantly deserves the support of the friends of the Society, and is one that, with God's blessing, will largely repay the toil expended upon it."

NEW MISSION HOUSE, VICTORIA, CALLED "BROOK MOUNT."

CHAPTER XV.

THE LAST DAYS IN AFRICA, 1870—1876.

HE last seven years of Mr. Saker's missionary life in Africa were years of steady and unceasing toil, often interrupted by sickness, and only varied by a short visit to England in 1874. The details of his daily work differ little from those already given, and it will suffice to select a few incidents that have some freshness or special interest.

Notwithstanding frequent exhaustion and growing weakness, he still pressed on his translations and labours at the press. On the 23rd of February, 1872, he announces the completion of the task he had set himself in the earliest days of his career. " I write you a line to-day with sensations of great joy. The great work of years is now completed, and I feel as a bird long imprisoned, liberated at last, with permission to fly and enjoy the glories of an open sky. I feel too much joy to express it in a few words. While I write this, do not think that the labour is all over and gone. There is yet much labour before us. Nevertheless, the victory is gained. The great work of getting into type this priceless boon to this country is now completed. The last sheet of the Sacred Volume, in good and readable type, is before me. There yet remains the task of reprinting such books as are much needed, and then binding the

10

whole in one volume. Our Bible will then be in three volumes—the Pentateuch, this volume, Joshua to Malachi, and the New Testament. This is mechanical toil, and will be done by my worthy helpers. Having thus prepared a tool, my own work henceforth will consist chiefly in preparing a body of young men and women to use it well. Four young men are now reading with me; two are already preachers, and the two others will, I hope, begin very soon. Then there are four others, younger, who are studious, working both at the type and their books. I have hope that God will call them also into His vineyard. These are in hand here. There are, beside the young men in the town, members of the church who have long been waiting for me to give them lessons, and my joy is not small that henceforth I shall have time to help them. On next Sabbath Day, we have the work of baptizing again. We hope our God has drawn seven others to Himself, and these we shall baptize and receive into the church."

But, although the translation of the whole Bible into Dualla was finished, he gave every spare moment to its revision. Often lying on his bed, strewed with his books, unable to rise, he pursued the study of the Divine records in the originals, noting the conclusions that his investigation led him to embrace. Referring to his studies in one of his letters, he says (April 25th, 1870), " I have been deeply interested for some weeks past in the writings of the old prophets. Would that I had more of their spirit. The more I look at those old Hebrew writings, the more majestic and amazing they appear; that so much should be said in such few words, that so much has been left unsaid such discrimination can only be Divine. While trans-

lating, I have often had to pause, being overwhelmed
with the revelation; and now, in printing, I feel again
my littleness, and am but a babe."

It was an additional cause of joy to Mr. Saker that an
American missionary from the Gaboon, visiting Cameroons in 1875, informed him that his Dualla version
of the Scriptures was perfectly understood by the
natives of that part of the coast.

The continual quarrels and wars among the tribes,
though often bringing the Mission families into great
peril, stimulated Mr. Saker's desire to spread among
them the gospel of peace. "The war," he says (writing
in November, 1872), "is not yet over. In fact, we
know not what will be spared to-morrow. Rifle balls
are flying about us, but at present our mission-house
and chapel are mercifully spared." Fearless amidst
every danger, he busied himself in repairing the damage
thus occasioned, in seeking to reconcile the combatants,
and in devising plans for the extension of the Gospel in
their midst.

The gift of a small steam launch, by a valued friend, on
his visit to England in 1874, gave hope to Mr. Saker that
he might be able to carry out the wish he had long
cherished of visiting the towns lying in the various
rivers that deliver their waters to the Cameroons.
Unexpected delays took place in its arrival. "I have
been strongly hoping," he says (July 17th, 1875), "that
this July mail would have brought my little boat. But
I must wait a little longer. I have no information
respecting it. From the time of my return till to-day,
I have given much attention to evangelistic labour
around us, as well as to printing. I am happy to say
that the work has been resumed at Bell Town, and the

10*

school established. At Malimba a school has been begun, and children already read in the first-class book, while one man evidences a change of heart. Others are seeking instruction. The more distant regions are still before me, like the land of Israel to Moses when on the mountains of Moab. Shall I, like him, be forbidden to enter the land? I have waited in perfect quiet, having my hands full, and shall find employment here if detained. But I long to do something more before I die. My general health is good, but I have to take all possible care, for the foe is ever on the watch to cast me down. Not a day passes but I hear the warning voice."

As the letter announcing the arrival of the long-desired boat is very characteristic, showing that the engineer of Devonport Dockyard had lost none of his early tastes or skill, it is given in full. The date is November 10th, 1875, from "Old Calabar":—"Before this reaches you, you will have learnt that the little steam yacht was left for me at this place, and that one of the traders kindly lent me the use of his boat to visit and take charge of it. I arrived here late on Friday night, the 5th inst. Since then I have been cleaning and finishing, for the engineers of the mail could not complete all they wished on account of time. I have put the little vessel on the beach, and, while the tide was out, accomplished all that was needful to be done except some rivetting in the paddle boxes, for which I need a forge. Last evening we again floated her into deep water, and to-day I have tested the engines. At high water I shall begin my homeward journey, but anchor at the mouth of the river all night.

" It is a small thing to say that I am very thankful

VIEW ON THE MUNGO RIVER—KROO BOYS COOKING BREAKFAST.

to receive this vessel after so long a delay. May it be a consecrated instrument to God's glorious work. I feel that its mission is one and simple—to bear the messenger safely and speedily to his distant work."

Between this date and the 10th of March (1876), Mr. Saker made three journeys in his little steamer; the third was one of intense pain and grief. Writing under date of February 28th, he says : " I left here (Cameroons) on the 17th. The next morning we sought to enter our eastern river for Lungarsi, but a tornado debarred us. Yet, as soon as possible, we steamed on, and managed to make some forty miles with comfort. The next day we went on again, but were soon detained by shallow water. We waited an hour, and then cleared the bank. Not more than thirty miles of progress all day. The next day was the Sabbath. Tried in the morning to reach the first village; found the water too shallow, so took the small boat to communicate with the people. Judge of my disappointment in finding the village to contain only five small huts, representing one family, and that a recent immigration from a higher settlement. The former people all cut off by the small-pox while I was in England.

"By the night tide we passed the bank which was our hindrance in the morning, and came again to deep water. Thence onward, and at nine in the morning made the Butu landing-place. We visited the people, examined the school-house; * it is now a ruin. It was abandoned on account of the plague, and has not been used since. Here I found all the old families gone. Two young men, sons of the former chief, welcomed us,

---

* At Malimba ; see before, p. 148.

and led us over the town, such as it is. I counted
fifteen houses, including the chief's three. At a later
hour I walked three-quarters of an hour through the
one-time town on the bank of the river. In that walk
I counted five huts, with two new ones building. I
heard of yet other huts if I would walk a mile
farther on. In all this walk the spoor of the hippo-
potamus and the elephant were everywhere. I cannot
describe the spiritless life of these few poor people.
The fearful visitation, cutting off such multitudes, is so
recent; stupefaction and powerlessness seem upon all.
We found some of the children alive who had read the
first class-book.

"After staying with these people four hours, we
passed a mile into 'Kotto.' It was here at Kotto that
my heart failed me; the desolation so great, so recent :
I met a man of years—the chief. With him I walked
over the ruins. The chief's street consists now of nine
separate buildings. Beyond, street after street, with
houses cast to the ground. In many streets not a house
left; the whole choked with *débris*, not a way to pass
through. Then we came to a house—solitary. It was
the house of a slave, the sole representative of a once
powerful clan. Then onward, and another house—the
home of a woman, the only survivor of a large family
which filled three streets. Then on and on, a heart-
rending sight. The one-time multitude to whom I
preached the good news of the Kingdom—where are
they ?

"Sadly I walked the length and breadth of that town.
The plantain and cocoa in luxuriant growth, and no
living owner; a land full of food, and the eater gone.

"I met in my walk seven men beside the chief, some

twenty women and grown girls, perhaps twenty-five children. Those I saw and those I heard of will give a population of about eighty souls. My estimate of the population on my former visit was four thousand!

"To these few grown-up yet broken men and women, what could I say? My own heart was dumb; an indescribable awe was upon me; I could do but little beyond commending them to God in prayer.

"After doing what we could at Butu and Kotto the Monday and Tuesday, we took the high water in the night, and passed safely over the banks on our return. Daylight came, and with tide and steam we went onward with speed, and that night anchored at the bar of the river in a terrible storm. It drifted us with our anchor and all our chain on to a large sand-bank, and nearly over it, and left us so high that we could only float off at nearly high water. Then an hour and fifteen minutes brought us home, thankful, yet sad. The words are constantly welling up within me, 'I was dumb, for Thou didst it.'"

Such are the terrible ravages of small-pox when it finds a nidus among an uncivilised people, far removed from all the remedies which civilisation can supply. Many a town on the coast of Africa has thus been wasted by this fatal and frightful disease.

From this time, the health of Mr. Saker steadily declined, and it became evident, towards the close of the year, that his shattered condition could no longer endure the fervid heats of the Torrid zone. One more visit to the interior, to the south of Bethel, was paid in the month of June, where he reports that he met with overflowing hearers. But he was compelled to say, "There is a general weakening going on. Daily I feel that the tabernacle is dissolving; hence I try to secure

every hour for such work as seems imperatively
demanded of me." Thirty-two years of labour in a
deadly climate, and the unresting toil in which he had
exhausted the energies of a frame always frail, left no
alternative if his life were to be prolonged for a single
day.

After his visit home in 1874, he had returned to
Africa with the Rev. J. Grenfell, a young man of
a congenial spirit and of youthful energy, to whom he
could confide the well-being of his beloved people at
Bethel; while at Victoria and on the mountain side, Mr.
Pinnock, and his son-in-law, Mr. Thomson, could watch
over his work and sustain the growing colony so dear
to his heart. Mr. Smith had died in the month of
August, in the prime of life; but Mr. Joseph Fuller was
admirably fitted to supply his place at Hickory and
Dido Town. In his last letter to the Mission House
from Africa, dated September 28th, 1876, after saying
that his "health has been failing very seriously," he
adds with joy, "I have good news from the interior;
the work of God is progressing there. Two other young
men will leave here in about three weeks for another
place where they are needed. Pray excuse more; my
head refuses to direct my pen." The end of this heroic
man's career in Africa had come, and it closed, as it had
begun, with the one absorbing thought and effort to
give to Africa the great salvation.

We cannot more appropriately bring this record of
an earnest missionary life to a close than by giving
Mr. Saker's own account of the work in which he
had been engaged, as narrated in a private letter to a
friend :—

"I cannot describe to you the condition in which I

found this whole people. A book they had not seen: the commonest implements of husbandry and tools of all kinds were unknown; civilisation, with all its appliances, was entirely absent. The hut for dwelling, and its separate shed for working, were in some respects objects beautiful to sight, and in their formation showed taste and ingenuity. Crockery, too, had just been introduced by traders, and bartered for oil. But these formed only objects for inspection and admiration to those who could not obtain them; they were the coveted possession of the chiefs.

"I brought with me tools to make my own dwelling. These attracted immediate attention, and soon several youths learned to use the saw, the plane, and the adze. The want of tools was felt by numbers, and I gave away much to meet that want. Implements of husbandry, the spade and the hoe, were introduced. Then I taught them to cut the large timber trees, and supplied the cross-cut and the pit saw, and aided them in sawing, till they could do it alone. I taught them better modes of culture, and planted ground as an example. I introduced seeds from other parts of the coast at a considerable charge, until the country was stocked with the sweet potato. And I had the pleasure of seeing a gradual extension of cultivation, and much less suffering from want. At our first settlement here, the total produce from the land did not exceed three months' consumption for the year, and there followed months of semi-starvation, and a running to distant places to purchase food at great expense. In the course of years we so improved that in some things there is now a redundance.

"In teaching these men various handicrafts and

husbandry, many wants were created, and, except from me, there was no means of meeting those wants. Hence I had to lend them tools, and nails, hinges, screws, locks, &c., &c., and this lending was, for a long time, no better than giving. In the course of time, and when the people were able to do it, I demanded a payment in produce, and accepted such a price as each was able to render. This also passed away, and now for a long time past I have (except in needy cases) exacted the full value of tools and other goods supplied; and, as we live chiefly by barter, we oft maintain our large family of native children by the exchange of nails, screws, hinges, &c.

"For all such expenditure you will readily see that the Mission funds are not available, and the attempt to supply the want was a heavy drain for years; indeed, my circumstances were for years on a level with the natives; our food was nearly the same; but we were clothed and they were not.

"Recalling thus the past, my heart again utters its glad thanks to those friends who aided me in the heavy expenses of those early years. Never shall I forget the relief I felt when a friend sent me £10 to buy seeds, or in any other way helped me on—in books, too, for those who learned to read and write, and in class and copy-books. I may also safely say that the many reams of note-paper I have consumed in translations, vocabularies, and grammars, friends have supplied the whole.

"Lest I weary you, I will now cease this reference to the past."

That these labours bore ample fruit in conversions, and in laying broad and deep the foundations of the Kingdom of God on this part of the coast of Africa, we have abundantly seen. Mr. Grenfell has assured us that, on the general population also, Mr. Saker's exertions were not without ample reward. When a palaver, or native council, he tells us, is held in the town, " the individual against whom a decision is given often refuses to accept the verdict, unless the native pastor or one of the deacons is in the majority. The knowledge that an adverse decision, if not endorsed by some of the Christian people, will be appealed against, renders the palaver especially attentive to their opinions. Culprits have great faith in the uprightness of the officers of the church, and feel sure that their judgment will be tempered by mercy. Such a fact speaks volumes for the power for good that the church possesses. Although the strife between the natives and the traders continues, the Mission premises are held to be neutral ground, and on Lord's-day both parties assemble in that home of peace, the house of prayer."

Thus, step by step, Christianity and civilisation have been planted, and the severe sufferings of Mr. Saker's early years have been abundantly repaid in the improved condition of the people and in the spread of Gospel light. Much yet remains to be done to banish the superstitions and bad habits that ages of ignorance have nurtured ; but the successors of Mr. Saker will find ready to their hand appliances which were vainly sought in the early stages of the work. The gains of the past are proofs that the Divine blessing has not been withheld, and are moreover pledges that greater things are in store to reward patient well-doing in the time to come.

Mr. Saker finally left the scene of his conflicts and successes by the mail of November, and reached his native land on the 12th of December, 1876.

CHAPTER XVI.

 LETTER dated the 12th of December, 1876, and written as the ship neared Liverpool, announced the arrival of Mr. Saker. "Dear brother," he said, "Thus far God has graciously brought us. In an hour I hope to land. The voyage home has been the renewal of my life. I shall land with much of my past health. This is a great mercy. Our voyage, though long (40 days), has been exceedingly pleasant. I have received every kindness and attention from the commander and officers, and much of my restoration is due to the comforts which have surrounded me." Although Mr. Saker wrote thus hopefully of his health, there awaited him many months of severe suffering. "The Shadow," as the natives of Cameroons had of late years been wont to designate him, as in weakness he moved about among them, landed, worn to skin and bone, emaciated to a degree scarcely conceivable, and with a constitution, never strong, now utterly broken. His indomitable spirit alone kept him alive. As the spring advanced, some degree of improvement began to appear, and in the early months of the following year he was able to visit, as a deputation, a few of the more important churches in various parts of the country.

The Mission to the Congo, which at this time was in

contemplation, excited his deepest interest, and in every possible way he rendered the aid that was in his power. His long acquaintance with equatorial Africa, its people and its languages, was of great service to the Committee, and made his counsel invaluable. Joyfully would he again have gone forth as the pioneer of this great enterprise. In a speech of rare merit that he delivered at Cannon Street Hotel, at the breakfast meeting held to expound the course taken by the Committee of the Society to inaugurate this Mission, after recounting some of the labours and successes of his life in Africa as grounds for encouragement, he added, with an "accent of conviction" that thrilled the assembly, "Though the years past have been years of suffering and years of toil, there is nothing in this country that could tempt me to stop—tempt me to exchange a life of labour and suffering there, if so be I can have but a repetition of the joy that has been given to me in that land. . . . . God hath accepted our past labours and blessed them. Let us in faith and in faithful labour trust Him for all the future."

In the year following, at the meeting held in Cannon Street Hotel to bid farewell to the four young brethren, Messrs. Comber, Crudgington, Bentley, and Hartland, who were about to enter on the Congo Mission, Mr. Saker met with a most enthusiastic reception, the whole audience rising to their feet to do him honour. In the following wise and devout language he gathered up the experience of his missionary life:—"While I congratulate you to-night, and the Committee also, in the establishment, so far, of this Mission, I should like to utter just this word—that the enthusiasm of this hour will not suffice. We are but beginning a work

which will test our fidelity, our faith, our zeal, and it
will test our hope also. Yet we may go forth with
confidence, because He that commandeth that we bear
the Gospel to the heathen hath Himself promised that
He will be with us. It is not prospective ; but He *is*
with us. 'Lo! I am with you always, even to the end
of the world.' And in the presence of the Master, and
armed with His power, your brethren, young as they
are, may go forth in confidence. You may send them
with confidence, and they will labour on faithfully and
successfully while they live near their Master, lowly,
trusting in Him, holding fast to His hand, and walking
as ever in His sight. But they may be called upon to
suffer. We know that they must labour, it may be long,
long years without much success, and in all the labour,
in all the suffering, in all the toil of the future, in all
the waiting, they will want your sympathy, your
prayers, your help : not the sympathy of this hour alone,
but the continuous sympathy of your hearts. These
brethren now going forth are but few, and they are
weak as we are ; yet in the hand of the Master they
can be strong. Pray, then, that the Master may not fail
them, that they may not fail their Master ; but that
they may live near unto Him, and that they work for
Him. And, then, while they are down in that deep
dungeon, you cannot know the sorrow, the suffering, the
toil, they may have. Keep hold of that rope, friends, on
which they depend. Let them have the consciousness
that the whole Christian heart of this country is beating
in sympathy with them, and that your prayers ascend
to the Master on His Throne that He may sustain them."

Once more, in the autumn of 1879, Mr. Saker
appeared before the delegates of the churches assembled

in Glasgow, and bore his testimony to the wondrous grace that had aided his labours, and prospered him in the work of the Lord. It was a wonderful sight to see that enfeebled man, that spare frame, that fading form, in tender, quiet, and yet thrilling words call forth the deep emotions of the vast throng gathered in St. Andrew's Hall. For several minutes he stood trembling with awe, as the assembly testified its regard and respect for the hero of the Cross. His last words were the breathing out of his life. "If," he said, "the African is a brother, should we not give him some of our bread and a draught of our water? Oh!" he exclaimed, with a glow of passionate feeling that touched and awoke into voiceful expression the chords of every heart in his audience, "that I had another life to go out there. The field is white there, the multitudes are in darkness still. It is the Son of God calling on us to go forth and preach the Gospel to this creature, and we have the promise that He will be with us unto the end. May His blessing be on you and on them."

Thus closed the public life of Alfred Saker. His few last months were cheered by the promise that his work at Cameroons would not be overlooked in the more exciting interest of the movement on the Congo. Mr. Comber and Mr. Grenfell had been taken away to devote their energies and their experience to the exigencies of the new field, but Mr. and Mrs. Lyall were accepted for King A'kwa's Town; and his son-in-law, Mr. Thomson, would not fail to watch with deep and anxious solicitude over the best interests of the colony of Victoria. Above all, his joy was full when the Committee accepted the services of his youngest daughter, Emily, that she might enter upon that portion of her father's

work which more especially concerned the training of
the young. From her childhood she had aided her
parents, and given, as the years went on, the most
efficient help to her father in his translations and printing work. Her familiar acquaintance with the Dualla
language was of great value to the Mission, and all
hearts were glad that the name of Saker would not be
lost or forgotten among the people he had lived to save.
I cannot refrain from quoting the following testimony
to the value of the labours of both father and child,
given by that eminent scholar, R. N. Cust, Esq., of the
Indian Civil Service, in his important and valuable
work (just published) on the Languages of Africa. " I
think also," he says, " of the patient, enthusiastic scholar,
often tried by fever and dysentery, and warned to fly,
yet lingering on until his work was stopped by death.
bearing hardships and discomforts of which we can
form no conception. And it is not every missionary
scholar who, like Saker, has left a young daughter
willing and able to take up the skein of an African
language dropped by her father, and carry through to
completion a revised edition of her father's translation
of the New Testament." * The mantle of the father
has fallen on his beloved child. Her parents, droop-
ing under the weakness and exhaustion consequent on
their long life in Africa, cheerfully relinquished " the
light of the house " for the cause of Christ in the Dark
Continent.

---

* "A Sketch of the Modern Languages of Africa," by R. N. Cust,
Esq., vol. i., p. 71. This edition of two thousand copies of the
Dualla New Testament was printed at the cost of the Bible
Translation Society. Though Miss Saker made many emenda-
tions of the text, it is rather a reprint than a revision.

During the last few months of his life, amid increasing suffering borne with singular patience with unabated mental clearness Mr. Saker would often return to his favourite occupations, and take up his Dualla vocabulary and grammar with the desire to render them more complete, or busy himself with his tools. But a single half-hour was sufficient to tire his worn-out powers, and for weeks he would be compelled to lay books and tools aside, sorrowfully sighing out the words, "Oh! what have I come to, that I cannot even do that?" He came home ill from Glasgow, and from that time the disease which he had so long manfully braved gained increasing strength. Reluctantly he was driven to decline the requests which reached him to visit various congregations where his presence would have been highly valued. With the cold winds of March (1880) he daily became more low. On the 8th of that month he had a very bad night, but in the morning slept a little. To his wife, who entered his room soon after he awoke, gazing at her with a far-off look, he said, "My dear, cannot we have a few words of prayer together?" Her heart sank; she felt that the hand of death was gently drawing him away. "He prayed," says the beloved partner of all his labours, "such a prayer as I had never heard. I often wish I could recall some of it, but I cannot. I felt, 'Truly God is here.'" He then slowly dressed, and descended to his room below, where he remained till the end came.

Nevertheless, he spoke hopefully to the doctor in attendance, and expressed the opinion that his work was not yet done. "No, my dear friend," was the reply, "it is not done, for I believe we shall have glorious

11

work to do yonder." " Yes," he answered ; " but I do not think my work for Africa is done yet." Nor is it done ; his works " do follow him," and the leaves of the tree of life he has planted on the Dark Continent remain still, and flourish for the healing of its people.

It was evident, however, to those who watched him with tender solicitude, that the shades of the dark valley were gathering over his head ; yet was the path before him lit up with the presence of Him who is the Light of Life and the Giver of Victory over Death. Calmly he comforted his wife with words of cheer and hope. " When God takes me," he said, " He will provide for you. Remember the past, through how many dangers and trials you have been brought. He will raise up friends for you."

As the evening of final rest drew near, he seemed at times scarcely conscious, and when he spoke it was with difficulty that he could be understood. Among his last distinct utterances was one addressed to his grandson Alfred. Seeing him entering the room to say " Good night," he watched the boy that he dearly loved to the foot of the bed, and then said, " God bless you, my boy." All day on Friday (the 12th) he was evidently yielding to the disease ; but it was not till about five o'clock in the afternoon that he fully realised that the end had come. He opened his eyes, and, looking earnestly at his wife, put out his hand for hers. She said, " Are you conscious that you are going to leave me ? " He nodded assent. " Are you quite happy ? " And again he gave the like token. Then closing his eyes, amidst much difficulty of breathing, gently and quietly, about one o'clock, he crossed the river of death. A sweet smile passed over the pallid, worn face as the ministering angels bore his spirit to the presence of his Lord.

In bringing to a conclusion this brief sketch of the life of Alfred Saker, I am happy to add the following additional particulars of the closing scene from the pen of my dear friend and successor, Mr. Alfred Henry Baynes, the present Secretary of the Baptist Missionary Society:—

" DEAR DR. UNDERHILL,—You have been good enough to ask me to give you a few particulars relating to the closing days of Alfred Saker's life. You know how our heroic friend disliked all titles; he often used to say to me, ' I will have neither prefix nor affix to my name—let it always stand, *Alfred Saker, Missionary to Africa.*' There was, as you so well know, a grand simplicity about our friend. He had an utter contempt for what the world calls ' fame.' I had the privilege of seeing him frequently during his closing days, and I regard those frequent pilgrimages of mine to Peckham as amongst the happiest memories of my life. Only a few days before he passed away, we were talking together of the probable opening up of Africa by the great Congo water-way. He was then lying in bed, seemingly little more than ' a bundle of bones,' and with scarcely enough skin to decently cover them, when he started up, and, looking at me with fixed eye, said, with intensest energy, ' Would I were a young man again, or had a second life to live, I would be off to Congo to-morrow.' He has told me more than once of how thoroughly Africa possessed his thoughts when he was quite a young man, and, when he was at work in the dockyard, with almost every stroke of the hammer on the rivet he fancied he heard

11*

the word '*Africa*' ring forth. At last he would become
wrought up to such a pitch that he could scarcely remain
at his work, in his passionate longing to be off. His one
master passion all through life was to live and labour for
the good of the Dark Continent.

"The last time I saw him alive—only a few hours
before his death—he was greatly exhausted, and I felt
sure the end was rapidly approaching. I can never
forget what took place then. He was speaking of how
manifestly Christ had been with him through the
night when, in great suffering, he thought his end
had come, and, turning to me with eyes full of
brightness, and with a voice unfaltering, he quoted the
words—

> ' Jesus, the very thought of Thee
>   With sweetness fills my breast ;
> But sweeter far Thy face to see,
>   And in Thy presence rest.'

And, apart from a 'Farewell,' and 'God bless you, my
dear friend,' these were his last words as I left the
house. A few more hours, and a final struggle, and
he passed through the gates into the city, and was for
ever at rest. Two days afterwards I stood by his coffin,
and looked upon his thin, pale, worn face—very peaceful and very calm ; it had lost much of its painful look,
the result of intense suffering, and there seemed resting
upon it a peace which was reposeful and beautiful. I
reverently bent my head down, and kissed his cold fore-
head, and said 'Farewell,' until the everlasting day dawn and
the shadows flee away, to one of the noblest grandest men
I ever expect to meet on earth, and I cannot recall that
moment without the deepest feeling of devout thanks-

giving that I was privileged to know him, and to call him *my friend.*

"Mrs. Saker will tell you that his last words were : 'For Thou art with me'; and surely these words tell out the whole story, and explain the entire life. A 'good soldier' of Jesus Christ, 'faithful unto death.'

"Oh, for grace, that we may be enabled to follow him, who now, through faith and patience, inherits the promises!"

On Friday morning, March 19th, at Nunhead Cemetery, amid sunshine and tears, the wasted frame of Alfred Saker was committed to the tomb, until the glad morning of resurrection. In the cemetery chapel, the Rev. C. M. Birrell read suitable portions of Scripture and offered prayer, and, after an address by myself, the Rev. J. P. Chown conducted the service at the grave. Many who loved him stood around the sepulchre, and sang, with devout and tender, yet grateful, sorrow, the singularly appropriate hymn—

> "Captain and Saviour of the host
> Of Christian chivalry !
> We bless Thee for our comrade true,
> Now summoned up to Thee.

> "We bless Thee for his every step
> In faithful following Thee ;
> And for his good fight fought so well,
> And crowned with victory.

> "We thank Thee that the wayworn sleeps
> The sleep in Jesus blest :
> The purified and ransomed soul
> Hath entered into rest.

> " We bless Thee that His humble love
> Hath met with such regard ;
> We bless Thee for his blessedness,
> And for his rich reward."

The sorrow felt in England had a touching and characteristic response in Africa. His native helper, Dibundu, writing to Mrs. Saker on hearing of the tidings of her beloved husband's departure, says:—" King A'kwa was up country when he heard of dear Mr. Saker's death. He was bitterly sorry, and all his people too; because they cannot forget all the good work Mr. Saker did in Cameroons river, and all round about. So the King made a law for his town, all of his own accord, in remembrance of Mr. Saker, that no work should be done on Sundays, but all ought to go to worship. So on Sunday, May 8th, all the people with one accord came to our chapel, which was over-full, and many more outside could not get in. You will remember us, please, in your prayers, that the good work may go on, and many be converted to Jesus."

Little more need be said respecting this true hero and faithful missionary of the Gospel of Christ. The narrative of his labours and the story of his life sufficiently express the spirit that animated him, and show the devotedness with which he wrought to fulfil his appointed service. He believed, with profound conviction, that the Lord of the harvest had summoned him to this task. Somewhat austere in manner, reticent in speech, untiring and indefatigable in the pursuit of the object he had set his heart upon accomplishing, he was, nevertheless, truly tender and affectionate in spirit. If he was hard to please by those who were laggards in the vineyard, or if his plans surpassed the apprehensions of those who were about him, he was ever the foremost in labour and the last to leave the field. He was the pioneer in a region in which he had no compeer, and to his hands fell the severe toil necessary to lay the foundations of the work he achieved. 'Take it all in all," is the testimony of that great man, Dr. Livingstone; "take it all in all, specially having regard to its many-sided character, the work of Alfred Saker at Cameroons and Victoria is, in my judgment, the most remarkable on the African coast."

Not less striking is the testimony of one of the most noted of modern African travellers, who visited the coast only a few years ago, with no sympathy for mission work, and no personal regard for Christianity: " I do not at all understand how the changes at Cameroons and Victoria have been brought about. Old sanguinary customs have, to a large extent, been abolished; witchcraft hides itself in the forest; the fetish superstition of the people is derided by old and young, and well-built houses are springing up on every hand. It is really marvellous to mark the change that has taken place in the natives in a few years only. From actual cannibals many have become honest, intelligent, well-skilled artisans. An elementary literature has been established, and the whole Bible translated into their own tongue, hitherto an unwritten one. There must surely be something ' abnormal' in this." *

Yes; but the " abnormal " character of Alfred Saker's labours lies in this: that, sustained by faith, with a heart quickened by the love of Christ, and inspired by the Holy Spirit of God, he wrought with full purpose

* *Missionary Herald* for 1880, p. 107.

of heart for the salvation of Africa, and God gave him the success that will ever attend the faithful servant of the Lord. His last words, " For Thou art with me," tell out and explain the story of his life. He was a good soldier of Jesus Christ, and, faithful unto death, and therefore he has won the crown of an enduring and immortal life.

Reader: Go, and do thou likewise.

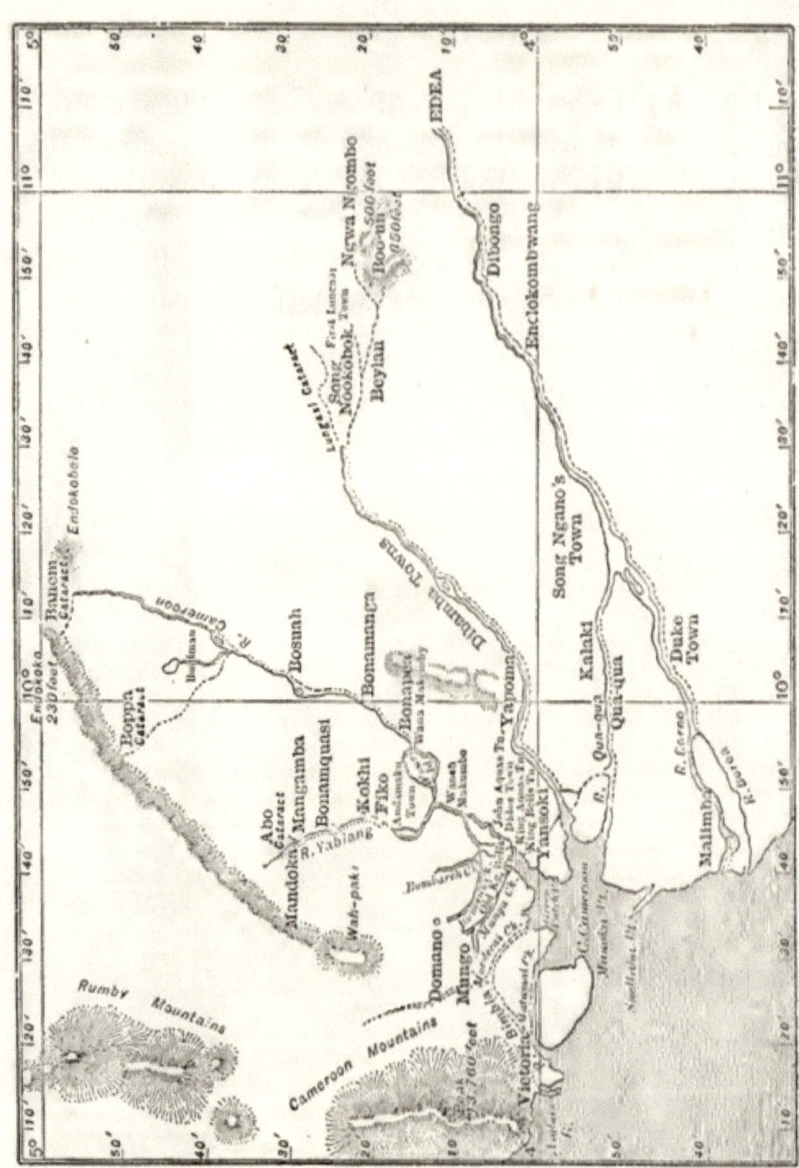

MAP OF CAMEROONS RIVER AND VICTORIA.

APPENDIX.

No. 1.

REGULATIONS FOR THE COLONY OF VICTORIA, AMBOISES BAY.

AGENCY OFFICE, *October*, 1858,
VICTORIA, WEST AFRICA.

This district, with its township now named Victoria, having **Victoria.** been purchased from the King of Bimbia, and the right and title thereto having been ceded to its present possessors ; and this township having been formed as a refuge and a home for those who cannot continue where liberty of worship is denied, and for all others who may be desirous of living peacefully with us, we do hereby arrange and decree as follows :

There shall be additional streets formed, as the wants of the township shall need them, according to the plan suspended in this office.

The spaces between the roads or streets shall be divided in **Lots.** building lots, and numbered. Each separate lot shall be a frontage of 50 feet and depth 100 feet.

These lots can be obtained, at this office, by expressed adhesion **How obtained.** to the regulations or bye-laws herein decreed and established among us this day ; and on the following terms :—

Firstly,—By PURCHASE, when a title for a secure possession will be given as a receipt of payment made, and an acknowledgment of the transfer.

Secondly,—By an AGREEMENT, for a nominal GROUND-RENT, and which agreement is to expire at the end of a term of—— years from date, with the option then of purchase at the market price, or a new agreement.

Thirdly,—By a FREE GRANT, to continue during the life of the recipients, man or wife, with then the option of purchase by the heir, at the market price, or a new grant to the children.

Possession. Any lot of ground in the township must be cleared of its bush and trees in six months, and a building—being a temporary or permanent house—must be erected thereon within the twelve months, and the roadways, measured by the frontage, kept cleaned. Failing in these preliminary steps, the right of possession lapses to this office, and the purchase money, if any, will be returned, but any expense incurred in a first clearing will be lost.

Garden ground. Garden ground in the neighbourhood granted to any settlers free for seven years.

For the sake of good order, health, and quiet, there must be cleanliness, sobriety, and a strict observance of the laws and regulations established among us, and which are as follows :

LAWS.

Officers. For the better security of the settlers, and for the suppression of disorderly conduct and crime, there shall be a Governor and a Council—the Governor being the owner of the estate or the representative of the owners.

Council. The Council to be composed of men of good character, and, if possible, of substance. This Council is not to exceed twelve persons; half to be chosen by the Governor, and half by the householders.

Duties. This Council shall have charge of all public roads and thoroughfares, of the beach and bays, and shall enforce cleaning of the roads and removal of all nuisances, summoning to their meeting all who infringe the laws in any way; and shall have power to inflict penalties not exceeding twenty shillings, or confinement with labour not exceeding one month.

Freedom of worship. There shall be entire freedom in all that relates to the worship of the true God; and the word of God is hereby acknowledged to be the foundation of all our laws, and claims the obedience of our lives.

That although we are now all of one mind in the essentials of Christian worship, yet should there come among us persons of differing opinions as to Christian worship or duty, all shall equally share in our freedom of worship, as well as in our protection.

That the worship of God be not interrupted, the Sabbath shall be regarded; all business shall be suspended, and the day esteemed sacred to worship and rest. *Sabbath.*

There shall be entire freedom in all that relates to trade and barter in the township and with the natives around. *Free trade.*

There shall be free importations of all goods, of provisions, of clothing, of trading goods, and machinery, of all and every article; except the following :

Rum, or other spirits, as articles of barter or sale, are for ever prohibited. *Prohibition*

Brandy, gin, and wine, admitted free for medicinal purposes, but for other purposes, not for sale or barter, only with a duty of ten per cent. paid on the value thereof.

Porter or ale, not for barter or sale, admitted————

Any infringement on the above clauses will involve, in all cases, confiscation of the property, and a fine of £5 sterling for the *first* offence; a fine of £10 sterling for the *second* offence; and expulsion for the *third* offence.

There shall be free exportation of all produce, live stock, or manufacture.

That the amount of imports and exports may be known, there shall be a registry kept at this office, and a true account must be delivered here specifying the amount or quantity of such imports or exports.

Power to institute and ordain laws against specific crimes and misdemeanours is reserved till occasion shall call for them. *Future laws*

All trees on this estate are the property of the owners; and while every facility will be afforded to settlers to obtain materials for building purposes in the township, no person shall be permitted to cut down or remove any tree for purposes of manufacture or exportation, except by written permission from this office, on payment of the assigned value, which will always be most liberal to settlers. *Property.*

APPENDIX.

No. 2.

RESOLUTION OF THE COMMITTEE OF THE BAPTIST MISSIONARY SOCIETY ON THE DEATH OF THE REV. ALFRED SAKER.

At the quarterly meeting of the Committee in April, the following resolution with regard to the decease of the Rev. Alfred Saker was unanimously adopted, and ordered to be recorded on the minutes of the Committee :—

"That the Committee of the Baptist Missionary Society cannot record the departure to his rest of the Rev. Alfred Saker without expressing in the warmest and most affectionate terms their high appreciation of his character and labours. For thirty-seven years Mr. Saker fulfilled his course as a missionary of the Cross in the exhausting climate of Western Africa, throughout suffering much from the diseases incident to a residence on that fever-stricken coast, yet never abating his toil nor intermitting his labours, though often physically unequal to the achievement of the task to which his life was given. He spared not his attenuated frame, nor did he retire from his post until utterly prostrate, and it was apparent to all that a further continuance was impossible. Under circumstances of great difficulty he planted the mission on the Continent, on the River Cameroons, induced the natives to abandon many of their sanguinary and degrading customs, and, by the blessing of God, established a church of Jesus Christ in their midst, ever to testify to the

grace and redeeming mercy of the Lord. With his own hands
he laboured to teach, and, encouraged by his example, he led the
people to acquire, the arts of civilised life ; he mastered, and for
the first time reduced to writing, their language ; prepared
school-books and grammar for their use, and crowned his
arduous labours by translating and printing the entire volume
of the Word of the living God. When the mission was driven
by the Roman Catholic Church from Fernando Po, he explored
the neighbouring coast, and founded the colony of Victoria in
Amboises Bay, where the converts gathered at Clarence might
find a refuge and a place to worship God without molestation, in
freedom of conscience, and exempt from further interference with
their personal rights and liberties. In every trial his resource
was the Mercy Seat, and, amid great provocations, he possessed
his soul in patience. He endured hardness as a good soldier of
Jesus Christ. He was faithful unto death. His whole life bore
record to the Psalmist's declaration, repeated in his last moments,
'For Thou art with me.' What he was God made him ; and
for his noble life, his heroic consecration, and blessed example,
the Committee adore the Divine Hand whose workmanship he
was.

"To his beloved widow and life-long companion in all his
labours and distresses, and the members of his family, especially
those who were his helpers in the work, the Committee tender
their earnest sympathy, and trust they may be sustained to the
end by the same Divine love, and cheered by the gracious consolation, which the Father of the fatherless and Husband of the
widow can impart to them in their sorrow."

www.ingramcontent.com/pod-product-compliance
Lightning Source LLC
Chambersburg PA
CBHW031955060726
47497CB00016B/2222